Also by Lisa Glatt

A Girl Becomes a Comma Like That

The Apple's Bruise

stories

Lisa Glatt

Simon & Schuster Paperbacks
NEW YORK · LONDON · TORONTO · SYDNEY

SIMON & SCHUSTER PAPERBACKS
Rockefeller Center
1230 Avenue of the Americas
New York, NY 10020

First Simon & Schuster paperback edition 2005

SIMON & SCHUSTER PAPERBACKS and colophon are registered trademarks of Simon & Schuster, Inc.

For information about special discounts for bulk purchases, please contact Simon & Schuster Special Sales: 1-800-456-6798 or business@simonandschuster.com

Manufactured in the United States of America

10 9 8 7 6 5 4 3 2 1

Library of Congress Cataloging-in-Publication Data
Glatt, Lisa.
    The apple's bruise : stories / Lisa Glatt.
        p. cm.
    Contents: Dirty Hannah gets hit by a car—The body shop—Animals—Tag—Soup—Bad girl on the curb—Grip—What Milton heard—Waste—Eggs—The study of lightning injury—Ludlow. I. Title.
PS3607.L375A86 2005
813'.54—dc22   2005042453

ISBN 0-7432-7052-5

Stories previously published: "Eggs," in *Pearl: A Literary Magazine*; also (under the title "ABC") in *Center: A Journal of the Literary Arts*. "The Study of Lightning Injury," in *Pearl*. "Animals," in *Center*. "Waste," in *Columbia: A Journal of Literature and Art*; also in *Best Woman's Erotica 2001* (Cleis Press) and *The Bust Guide to the New Girl Order* (Penguin Books). "Grip" and "Tag," in *Indiana Review*. "Soup," in *Indiana Review*; also in *Swink*. "What Milton Heard," in *Prism International: Contemporary Writing from Canada and Around the World*. "Bad Girl on the Curb," in *Another City: Writing from Los Angeles* (City Lights Publishers). "Ludlow," in *Women on the Edge: An Anthology of L.A. Women Writers* (The Toby Press). "The Body Shop," in *Zoetrope*.

For David

Contents

Dirty Hannah Gets Hit by a Car

1.

HANNAH LIVES IN A SOUTHERN CALIFORNIA BEACH CITY without sidewalks, with lawns and flowerbeds that go right down to the curbs, and today, because it is Monday, trash day, those curbs are lined with fat green bags and reeking metal bins. And today, because her parents are fighting, she will walk across the street, stand on Erika Huff's porch, and knock on the front door. And today, because Erika is sick, Hannah will walk to school alone.

Erika is two years older than Hannah and only talks to her when no one's looking. She's more doll than girl, Hannah's decided, with her huge, gray eyes that rarely seem to blink. Her hair is long and blond and shiny. It swishes when she walks. Hannah's dark, tight curls do not swish.

On mornings just like this morning, Hannah has stood on the Huffs' porch, waiting, staring down at the welcome mat with her bagged lunch knocking at her hip, overhearing Erika's protests. "Not again. Forget it. I won't touch her—we look like lezzies." And she has heard Mrs. Huff groan and beg. "Please, Erika. Please, honey." And Erika responding with *no, no, no,* and then the words that echo down the foyer. "She's dirty, Mom. I won't hold her hand."

"Not so *loud,* Erika. The poor girl will hear you," Mrs. Huff scolds.

"She's dirty," Erika insists.

Always, Mrs. Huff says then, "The girl is all alone in the world" or maybe she says, "all along in the world"—but either way Hannah knows from the woman's tone that *all along* or *all alone* makes her a girl to be pitied.

She has glanced at her plastic watch and feared Mr. Henderson's reprimand about being tardy, imagined him bending down, face inches from her face, saying, "Hannah Teller, you're late. *Again,* Hannah Teller." She has peered through the crack in the front door and into the kitchen where Mrs. Huff stands with a hand on her hip, sighing loud enough for Hannah to hear. She's watched the woman move out of the room, out of her view, and return within seconds, clutching her red purse under her arm. She smacks the purse down on the counter, unzips it, and pulls out her wallet, saying "I'll pay you. You happy now? Feel good about yourself? What kind of a girl are you?"

Erika shrugs and sneers—even from the doorway, Hannah has seen her shoulders rising, her lips twisting.

Mrs. Huff snaps open the wallet then and the green bills move from her hand into her daughter's waiting palm. "You're a Christian girl," she says. "You should behave that way."

Soon, Erika joins Hannah on the porch and defiantly snatches her hand, muttering under her breath, almost dragging her down the driveway. And Mrs. Huff shouts after the two of them. "Be nice, girls. Be good girls."

When they get halfway down the block and out of Mrs. Huff's view, Erika drops her hand and wipes off her own, slapping her palm against her skirt or jeans as if whatever makes Hannah awkward and unpopular might very well be contagious.

Today, though, Erika is the one who's contagious, sick with red blisters on her face and body that Mrs. Huff describes to Hannah in theatrical detail. "There's one the size of a pancake covering her belly, and four shaped like almonds on her face. It's the strangest thing. They go like this," Mrs. Huff says, using a manicured nail to sketch a perfect C on her own cheek.

"Oh," Hannah says quietly.

"And she won't stop scratching," she continues. "You know Erika—she does what she wants. It's what she wants or it's nothing at all. She's like her father that way. When she was little she wouldn't even eat ice cream. Imagine that."

Hannah's nervous, biting her bottom lip.

"Anyway, now she's making herself bleed. The sores are oozing—the rash spreading. It's terrible."

"Sounds bad," Hannah says.

"The doctor says it's not chicken pox and they're not any hives he recognizes. What do we pay him for?"

Hannah looks at her blankly.

"You know Erika," she says. "You know it's her way or the highway. If she wants to scratch, she's going to scratch. You know Erika," she says again.

"I guess," Hannah says quietly.

Mrs. Huff wipes her hands off on her apron and bends down. "Look, honey," she says, "I know your mother and father are having . . . well, problems." She says these last words in a whisper, leaning closer, even though it's just Hannah on the porch. "Maybe your parents can take you to school. Tell your mother that Erika is sick and can't walk with you today. Tell her about the rash. Okay, sweetie?"

And Hannah lies and nods and tries to smile, then turns away from Mrs. Huff and heads back across the street to her own home, where she's certain that her mother and father are deep inside their argument.

Her parents' fights are so loud and physical and public— doors slam, plates or cups take flight, her mother screeches away in the sedan, and two Saturdays ago, her father punched a hole in the living room window. Hours later, with one hand bandaged, he pulled strip after strip of duct tape, stretching those strips from one jagged edge to the other until the hole was covered. He muttered about temporary solutions, trapped birds and bad weather, then turned to the couch, where Hannah was sitting with an open coloring book in her lap.

"This won't necessarily keep the killers out, but it'll at least cut down on the chill," he said.

She looked up at him, afraid.

"Don't listen to me," he said.

"What killers?"

"I meant to say thieves—the ganif."

"What killers?" she said again.

"The new window arrives tomorrow morning," he tried.

"Sometimes thieves are killers, too."

Her dad laughed then. "You're just too smart," he said. "I'm sorry, Hannah." He stood there with his back against the patched-up window, shaking his head. His injured right hand hung at his side and he wore the cardboard roll like a bracelet on his left wrist. "I'm sorry," he said again, coming over and sitting down next to her. He let the cardboard roll slip from his wrist onto the coffee table, where it bounced a couple of times before ending up next to her box of crayons. "Sometimes you accept your life, what you've made of it, your choices, and sometimes, well—" He stopped himself and looked at the open book in her lap. "What do you got there? What are you coloring?"

On the page there was a sun Hannah had colored bright blue. There was a girl jumping rope whose skin she'd made green. And there was a trio of trees she had just begun to think about. "Interesting," her father said. "Not the colors I'd expect, but you're good at staying in the lines, Bubele. You're careful, cautious."

And Hannah will need those very skills today when she crosses the streets on her own, but right now she's heading up the driveway, alongside her mom's sedan, hoping that when she turns around, Mrs. Huff will have closed the front door and disappeared. She has no intention of actually *going* home, of walking inside the house and interrupting her parents, but when she turns around and sees Mrs. Huff with her hands inside her apron pockets still looking at her, she grabs hold of the doorknob and twists. And only when the door opens does Mrs. Huff give her a wave and finally go away. Still, Hannah doesn't enter the house, just pops her head and neck inside, like a criminal, like a thief or killer casing the place, or like a girl who doesn't even live there with those people but wants to know what all the ruckus is about.

Her parents stand in the kitchen, screaming, her mother repeating that forbidden word, "fuck, fuck you and fuck your lies and fuck your shikse. Fuck your train ride. You *needed* to be alone. You *had* to be alone. Who's alone in wine country? Who takes a train to Monterey and sips expensive Cabernet by himself? What kind of a fool do you think you married, Asher?" She has the hand-painted bowl they brought home from Ojai last year in her hand, holds it high above her head and aims it at the wall or maybe at Hannah's father, whose head Hannah can only see half of, but whose voice she hears whole; it booms out of his mouth. "Put down the bowl. Stop this mishegas. You're crazy," he screams.

She closes the front door quietly and decides to walk to school on her own. She knows the way to Washington Elementary. Three blocks straight ahead, cross one street, pass the cul-de-sac, cross another street, and make a quick left.

· · ·

Mrs. Huff was right about one thing: Hannah *knows* Erika or maybe it's that Erika knows her. Last month, because Erika's best friend Millicent was away for the weekend, Erika knocked on Hannah's front door with a bag of chocolates and asked her to play. It was mid-afternoon, a Saturday, and Erika Huff was on Hannah's porch, and behind her the sun was a fat, yellow ball. The sky was clear, blue everywhere, not one cloud. Hannah could even see the mountains from behind Erika's head.

"My dad just cleaned the pool. Let's go swimming," Hannah suggested, excited.

"I've got a pool of my own, Teller."

"Oh."

"I don't need your pool."

"How about—" Hannah began, but Erika cut her off.

"Let's go somewhere dark. I've got chocolates. We can sit somewhere and tell ghost stories."

"Ghost stories?"

"It'll be fun."

"Swimming is fun, too."

"Not as fun as telling stories in the dark. You like chocolates, right? All girls like chocolate."

So Hannah led her into the garage.

All afternoon she lay on an old cot while Erika ordered her around and did things to her. She told her to lift up her shirt, and Hannah obeyed. She told her to leave the fabric over her face, and she did it. She told her to stay quiet while she pinched Hannah's skin, her neck, her shoulder, the baby-fat fold where her underarm meets the side of her chest. She told her to take off her jeans without sitting up, and Hannah wriggled right out of them. She told her to open her legs so she could get to the tender skin inside her thighs.

"Stay still," she said. "Don't move, Teller."

Hannah heard her unwrapping the piece of chocolate candy, the crinkling of cellophane. Though her face was covered and the garage was dim, she saw Erika's shadow as she popped a piece in her mouth, her cheeks fat with sweetness then, and she was talking through the candy, saying, "None for you, Hannah. It's all mine."

Hannah smelled gas, and on the shelf to her left she could barely make out the red can her father kept for emergencies.

"Delicious. None for you," Erika said again.

Hannah wasn't even that hungry. She'd get a treat from her mother later. Maybe her dad would take her out for ice cream.

"They're special chocolates, from France," Erika continued, "and they're only for girls like me."

Early the next morning Hannah's mother stood at her bedroom door with the laundry basket balanced at her hip. "Where did those bruises come from?" she said.

Hannah rubbed her eyes. "Huh?"

"On your arms." She set the laundry basket down and moved toward Hannah's bed.

"I fell off my bike," she lied.

"You okay, honey?"

"I'm sleepy."

"When did this happen?"

"Yesterday."

"You didn't go for a bike ride yesterday. When did you have time?"

Hannah said nothing.

"I picked you up from school and we went shopping, honey. I bought you new shoes and socks, remember? That pretty white blouse?"

"Maybe it happened a couple days ago."

Her mother looked at her, confused.

"It doesn't matter," Hannah said.

"Okay, sweetie."

If she were a better girl, honest, Hannah might have told her mother the truth, that all she wanted was a friend, but she stayed quiet, pulled the sleeves of her nightgown down over the bruises, and felt her eyes welling up. She turned from her mother and stared at the wall.

"It's okay," her mother said again, her voice soft. She leaned down and smoothed the hair away from Hannah's face. "You'll be more careful next time—I know you will," she said.

Today Hannah's trying to be careful, avoiding those fat trash bags and metal bins, walking on the neighbors' lawns, stepping as lightly as she can. And she's okay, feeling grown-up and independent. Perhaps she *is* what Mr. Henderson says she is: a problem solver. Perhaps she will, as her mother has promised, grow into someone confident and graceful. Perhaps her house will fill with girls who do not want to pinch her—girls who will want to go for a swim.

As she's nearing the intersection, she hears her. "Little girl, get off my lawn," the woman yells.

Hannah pretends she doesn't hear her, though, the way she sometimes sits with her back against her bedroom door, pretending not to hear her parents, the way she pretends she doesn't hear Erika call her dirty. With only a few feet left, she thinks she can surely make it, one step and then another and then a couple more, but now the woman's voice again, gravelly and thick, louder this time, so loud it demands Hannah turn around and face her. And there she is in her pink robe, holding the front door open with a plump hip. There she is with a cigarette between her lips, the cigarette bobbing up and down as she yells. "Get off my lawn. You hear me? You deaf?"

And Hannah is many things, but deaf is not one of them.

She is fearful, afraid of dogs and bugs and even some plants. The dark green bushes in front of her dotted with red berries—they're scary. And across the street that huge German shepherd chained behind the picket fence is scary, too.

She is short, the second shortest in her class, only taller than Eddie Epstein, who's confided in her that he's on medicine that's supposed to help him grow. Eddie is a nice boy, a boy that asks about her weekend, but still Hannah's very afraid that those pills might work. While Mr. Henderson writes the spelling words on the chalkboard she often stares at Eddie, who sits right next to her. His little tennis shoes and jeans, his T-shirt, his delicate shoulders, the miniature denim jacket hanging over the back of his chair. She imagines Eddie growing and growing, sprouting right out of his desk, taller and taller, passing the huge and handsome Tyler twins, passing the chalkboard, passing Mr. Henderson too, until Eddie's head brushes the ceiling, until he leaves Hannah behind.

She is timid—her mouth is like that broken window, sealed with duct tape. She doesn't shout out or complain when she should. Like right now. Like that woman's voice again. "Get *off* my lawn, little girl." Hannah knows, like she knew in the garage with Erika, that to shout back or speak up is the right thing, the only thing to do really, and still she remains quiet, her lips shut as if with paste.

And here, in front of her, are her two obedient feet, one black, shiny shoe stepping out and the other one following. She accidentally steps on a bunch of those red berries she's afraid of, smashing them, leaving a red footprint with each subsequent step. And the dog barks and barks, he growls and runs toward the fence, but the chain yanks him back into the yard, and for a second he's on two legs, dancing and more fierce than ever. She steps off the curb and into the street, aware of her heart and lungs, her own breathing. She's aware of the wind too, which has picked up—and her face damp with sweat. She walks around the trash cans, curling around them carefully, despite their smell, her body so close without actually touching them. She's wearing her blue plaid jumper and new cotton blouse, little white socks with lacy edges. She has a stretchy headband on her just-washed hair. What is Erika talking about? she thinks. She's not dirty Hannah. She's not dirty at all.

2.

Hannah lives through the accident, but loses things: her spleen, half of her calf muscle, the baby toe from her left foot, which her father will look for and never find. She loses the last two months of second grade and the memory of the car itself, although her parents will tell her later what it looked like: a red bug, a Goddamn Volkswagen, they'll say.

Now, her parents stand on opposite sides of the hospital bed, her father holding a ceramic lamb with fake flowers and plastic green leaves shooting out of its back. A present for Hannah. She's supposed to like it. And her father's head has a gash that points one way and then another, or maybe it's two gashes—yes, yes, Hannah sees now, two distinct lines that are so red and thick and fresh, that the skinny, freckled nurse wonders out loud if he was the one driving the car that hit her.

"He's Hannah's father," her mother says, angrily. "Can't you see?" she asks the nurse, who only shrugs, then leans down and fiddles with the dial on Hannah's IV bag before pointing at her father. "What about his head? What happened there?"

Hannah's father sighs.

"He hurt himself," her mother says, leaning close to the nurse's chest, getting a look at her nametag. "He ran into a wall, Betsy."

"You should really have that looked at." Betsy's eyes narrow and she moves toward him.

"He's fine," Hannah's mother snaps, waving her wrist, shooing the nurse away.

"Doesn't look fine to me," the nurse snaps back. "I'm a nurse," she says, stating the obvious, "and he looks anything *but* fine."

Hannah's father shakes his head. He sighs again. He puts the ceramic lamb down on the nightstand, reaches for Hannah's hand and holds it.

"I know what you are, Betsy." Her mother's voice cracks. She reaches into her purse, pulls out a tissue, and begins to cry.

"I'll just leave the three of you alone," Betsy says, obviously embarrassed. "If you need anything, Hannah, just ring that buzzer like I showed you," she says, sweetly, before turning her back and walking away.

Hannah's dad walks over to her mother's side and puts his arm around her waist. "She'll be okay," he says, soothingly. "We'll all be okay," he tells her mother, who blows her nose then, honking into the tissue, shaking her head no. "I need a pill, Asher," she says. "I need something to get me through this."

"We'll pull together," he says.

"Look at my baby—her leg is in traction and where is her toe? Can you tell me, Ash, where is my daughter's toe?"

Hannah's father's eyes well up.

"I need a pill," she says again.

Later, years later, Hannah will learn that the bowl hit her father's cheek, cracked in half, and cut him open in two spots. And she will learn that her father was already a man cut in two, that he loved a woman in a city just east of theirs, that he loved her three Persian cats as if they were his own, that his heart had been divided before Hannah was even born.

3.

After they remove her spleen, Hannah's improvement is quick and steady, and the doctors seem to like her. They walk into her room together in pairs, acknowledging her with wide smiles. "You'll have a story to tell the kids at school," the tall one says. "You're sure a trouper," the pudgy one tells her. "She's seven going on seventy. A mature girl. A smart girl. A very old soul," the tall one adds.

By week three, though, Hannah's temperature suddenly spikes and the doctors seem frustrated. She's not so smart or mature anymore. She's crying like the baby she is. And she was doing so well. What happened to her? They look at Hannah like she's done something wrong, like maybe she knows what's killing her and is choosing to keep it a secret. "Where does it hurt?" they ask repeatedly. One scratches his head. The pudgy one tugs on his beard. He leans in, close enough for Hannah to feel his hot breath on her hot face, for her to smell whatever pungent thing he ate for lunch.

"Everywhere," she answers.

"*Everywhere?*" he says, exasperated.

"And nowhere," she tells him, truthfully.

Back in ICU she's sweating and hallucinating. She doesn't know what's real and what isn't. Her parents visit her now individually, one at a time, her weepy mother during the day and her stoic father in the evenings, or maybe it's the other way around; she can't be sure of anything. Maybe the gash on her father's head is closing up, healing as it should be healing, or maybe time is moving backwards and the wound is open-ing up again, the skin pulling apart. Perhaps Mrs. Huff and Erika come by or perhaps they don't. Maybe they're ushered away by two stern nurses. Maybe that was Erika's small figure and waving hand in the doorway or maybe it was an oversized doll.

Test after test.

Drink this chalky mixture. Pretend it's a milk shake.

X-rays.

Handfuls of colorful pills.

That's right, swallow them all. No, no, all of them. Come on, Hannah. Be a good girl. You want to get better, don't you?

More tests.

The pudgy doctor's pudgy finger in her ass.

And nothing.

Until a new doctor arrives, who's young and lean, with jeans under his white jacket and a degree, Hannah's mother tells her, from Stanford. He wants them both to call him Dr. Seth and he's smarter than the rest, she says, smiling for the first time in weeks, fixing her hair, poofing it up with her fingers. Dr. Seth believes Hannah's liver is abscessed, even if the last three tests came back negative. "It's most likely in a place we can't see, a spot the scans didn't pick up," he says, picking up her mother's hand to demonstrate. "Here's what we saw in our first few X-rays, the front of the liver and the back, too," he says, tapping gently on her mother's fingernails, which are shiny and red, newly painted, Hannah can tell. "And here's the underside." He flips her hand over in his own and stares a second at her palm. "We'll know more this afternoon," he assures them both.

And now it's 3:00 a.m. and the rushing nurses tell Hannah nothing about what they know. They insert a new IV into her wrist. They lift her from the bed onto a gurney. They hurry her down the hall and into the elevator where, despite the excitement, she watches the numbers light up and her eyes grow heavy.

When she wakes up, there's a thick tube snaking from her right side and across the room, spewing the infection into a huge machine that Dr. Seth says is cleaning her out, which reminds Hannah of Erika calling her dirty, and maybe, she thinks to herself, Erika was right after all.

4.

She's been hooked up to the liver-draining machine for three days and her fever disappears and her cheeks are pink and her appetite is back. She eats plates of unrecognizable meat and the palest, softest vegetables and blue Jell-O or red Jell-O and little cups of ice cream that she opens herself, pulling the tab. They've moved her downstairs to the floor where the kids are just sick, not necessarily dying, her mother tells her. "You're not dying, you're going to be fine, Hannah, I'm so grateful," her mother says—all of her words rushing together.

When Dr. Seth enters the room, she looks up at him and fixes her hair with her fingers again. Hannah looks to the mute television hanging from the ceiling and turns up the volume and switches channels, impatiently, madly, until her mother asks what's wrong with her.

"A lot," she says, surprising herself.

She looks at Hannah, perplexed.

"I'm in the hospital, aren't I?"

"That's right, honey," she says, sweetly now, attentive again. "That's right."

5.

Mrs. Huff and Erika arrive on a Sunday afternoon. They've been to church. They've heard a wonderful sermon. "Can't get Pastor Mike's words out of my head. What a man. What *conviction*," Mrs. Huff says. She carries a plate of chocolate chip cookies and a stuffed bunny rabbit, which Hannah wishes wasn't such a baby gift, but still she thanks her. "What you've been through," Mrs. Huff says, shaking her head. She sets the cookies on the nightstand, then leans forward and slips the bunny rabbit under Hannah's blanket and actually tucks it in. "Cookies are straight out of the oven—or they were this morning, before church," Mrs. Huff says. Erika stands in the doorway, staring at the tube snaking out from under Hannah's sheet, and looks horrified, afraid to even enter the room.

"Come here," her mother says. "Come over and say hello to Hannah."

Erika shakes her head, but it's not a protest that Hannah

17

recognizes, there's no sneering involved, no strength or anger, only fear.

"Come on in," Hannah says.

Erika just stands there.

"Don't be a chicken," Hannah insists.

Mrs. Huff looks at Hannah, surprised. "Dear, let's not be mean. This is Erika's first time in a hospital, you know."

"I didn't know that."

"You do now," she says, straightening her skirt.

"But I *didn't* know," Hannah insists, ready to fight.

"Whatever you say, honey," Mrs. Huff says, backing down. "You're the one who's sick here. You need all the love and prayers you can get. We've been praying for you. Isn't that right, Erika?" she says, turning to her daughter.

Erika says nothing. She's biting her nails and looks as if she's about to cry.

"It's *my* first time in a hospital, too," Hannah tells them.

"But you've been here a while—you're used to it," she says brightly.

"I'm not used to it."

Mrs. Huff gives her a weak smile, then turns to Erika again. "Get over here," she says sternly. "Now," she nearly shouts.

Erika takes one meek step and then another until she's in the middle of the room, looking down at her shoes. And Hannah is thinking of the steps Erika's taken in the past, the bounce and bully in them. She's thinking about the time Erika snatched a turkey sandwich right from her hand when she passed Hannah in the lunchroom. Erika was walking with Millicent, and Millicent was walking with Erika, the way girlfriends walk together, the two of them talking and giggling behind their cupped hands, and then Erika's hand swooped down like a vulture and snatched the sandwich. The bread was white and soft and fresh, Hannah remembers, and the sandwich was just an inch or two from her mouth, and she was hungry, ready for that first bite, salivating, and then, then it wasn't hers anymore.

And instead of rising from that bench, shouting out or telling the lunch monitor, Hannah's eyes shot around the room, hoping that no one else witnessed her surprise and humiliation. She picked up the apple from her napkin and without looking at it, took a big, violent bite, juice cascading down both sides of her mouth. She bit right into the apple's bruise and chewed and chewed, pretending she loved it, pretending that soft brown spot was the very thing she was hungry for, the very thing she craved.

"Closer," Mrs. Huff insists now. "Get over here," she says.

More meek steps and then Erika's at Hannah's bedside, her fingers curled around the metal bar that makes the bed look like a giant crib. She's just inches from the tube and obviously mesmerized.

"My liver was abscessed," Hannah says, matter-of-factly. "An abscess is a really bad infection."

Erika shudders.

"It was invisible to most of them. I mean, the doctors didn't know it was even there. But Dr. Seth found it. My liver was full of pus," Hannah continues, enjoying Erika's discomfort. "Gross, huh?"

Erika steps back, away from the bed.

Mrs. Huff pulls on the girl's sweater. "Stay here," she whispers harshly into Erika's ear.

Hannah looks at Erika's face and sees the scars then, four of them, almond-shaped, just as her mother described. Hannah remembers the morning of the accident, standing on the porch while Mrs. Huff sketched that C on her own face. The scars are thick and oily. Hannah knows she should look away, focus on Erika's big doll eyes or ask about her sweater, which is probably new, but she doesn't.

"We put some vitamin E oil on the scars this morning, didn't we?" Mrs. Huff says. "Erika did it herself. Punctured the pill with a pin, squirted the oil onto some gauze like her own little nurse. Didn't you, honey?"

Erika nods, sheepishly.

"The scars are temporary. You won't even see them in a few months." She clears her throat. She clears her throat again. "They'll go away, Hannah," she says slowly, her voice firm.

Hannah looks at the bunny next to her, its stupid pink head sticking out from under the blanket.

"She'll be just as pretty as she's always been," Mrs. Huff says. And Hannah knows that she's trying to tell her something else too, something about things returning to the way they were, and Hannah feels warned. She looks back at Erika's face and is ready to speak up, protest, when Dr. Seth knocks on the open door and flashes that smile.

He looks good, Dr. Seth, even better than usual, with his white coat unbuttoned, his slim hips and jeans, the stethoscope hanging in front of his own heart, and Mrs. Huff suddenly perks up. She seems to have forgotten about her daughter's scarred face and what she was trying to say. She's touching her own swishy hair with her fingers and smiling at Dr. Seth. Erika skitters away, stands again in the doorway with that frightened look on her face.

Dr. Seth gives Erika and Mrs. Huff a perfunctory nod but focuses on Hannah. "How are you doing, Han? You feeling better?" And then he's leaning down and taking her hand, the one without the IV, and then he's kissing that hand, and she feels proud and popular. "That tube's about done its job," he tells her. "You're just about all cleaned out," he says, smiling.

And Hannah is smiling too, then looking back at Erika, who's moved out of the doorway and into the hall, where she stands biting her nails again. Hannah's remembering that sandwich she didn't get to eat, the bruises, and the chocolates Erika didn't share.

Later, hours later, Dr. Seth will trick her. He'll tell her to look at the bird outside the window, the bluebird sitting on a branch, and when Hannah's looking, when she's staring right into the bird's tiny face, he'll yank the tube out in one swift and painful pull. She'll hate him, crying as he bandages the hole left in her side, but now, now she almost loves him.

"It's been traumatic—what she's been through," he tells Mrs. Huff, who's grinning like an idiot.

And Hannah thinks again about Erika's cheek, those thick

21

scars, the C the two of them know will always be there, and says to her, "Come on in, Erika. Come back here. I don't bite," she tells her, thinking that maybe she *does* bite, that maybe she's becoming just that sort of girl.

The Body Shop

THERE ARE FACTS, CERTAINLY: THAT IN APRIL MY HUSBAND carried the stripper off the stage and sobbed in her arms, that it's mid-May now and we're separated, and that months ago, just after her twentieth birthday, our daughter Tessa broke out of rehab with a man more than three times her age, drove with him across the country, and now lives with him in a shack in Maine—no phone, no electricity, and no running water. I'll see you when I see you, she said from a pay phone in Arizona. I've got my own life to live, she told us from Texas. And from Kentucky, Do you think your lives are any better?

In addition to the facts, there are the scenes I imagine, like my girl climbing on the man's feeble back and hoisting herself out a window, though it's most likely the two of them just left that hospital on a hill, walked out the front door holding hands, Tessa and her old man, and into the bright day.

And when I think of that night in April, that night I've only heard about and pieced together, the details are sharp, even if inaccurate. I see the stripper's arms wrapped around my husband, when, in fact, she was unwillingly there, and those arms hung impotently at her sides until she made use of them and pushed my husband away. It was midnight when Robert, only halfway through his crying jag, was tossed out of the place finally like so much trash.

He carried her off the stage in front of all of them: the other patrons, the bartender who froze with his bottle tilted in the air above a glass, and the other strippers too, who'd heard the commotion and risen from their stools and mirrors, who traveled in a curious group over to the curtain and stood behind it, whispering to each other about Robert, one of the regulars, an ordinary guy really or so they thought. It was Little Girl Night, and the little girls who were really grown women stood there, one dressed up as a cheerleader, one a Catholic, a redhead on roller skates. All of them were aghast, but only the cheerleader stepped through the curtain, onto the stage, and aimed her pom-pom at the back of my husband's head. She missed, barely clipping his elbow, but it didn't matter by then because he was oblivious, determined, and Scarlet was bent over his shoulder and slapping at his back with open palms. Someone in the audience called for the bouncer, who at that very moment was reclining after four hours of oral surgery on a cot in the back of the club.

My husband was a spectacle. He fell into that stripper's reluctant arms, her appalled arms, her arms that gave him a brief respite, two minutes tops—more out of shock than sympathy—and then those arms rightfully pushed him away.

I paid a lot of money to watch those girls dance, my husband said, defending himself.

And take off their clothes, I added.

Yes, he said.

My money, I said.

What?

It was my money you spent at The Body Shop, Robert. I'm the only one working.

Oh, *that* now.

Yes, *that*.

I'm just saying.

You're not saying anything.

You can't hear me, Megan, he said.

I'm right here, I said. Ears open. Listening.

Right, he said.

Say something discernible, I said. Make some sense. Try to tell me why you did it.

I couldn't help it, he said.

That's what your daughter said in seventh grade. What she might say now if we asked her why she's off with Pops. You can do better than that. Please, do better, Robert.

I couldn't help it, he said again.

Don't say that. That's embarrassing.

See?

See what?

Nothing, he said.

What were you *thinking?* I repeated.

He told me he didn't want to fuck her, but moved onto the stage and carried her away because of something else, something he couldn't yet articulate. That wasn't enough for me.

Try, I said. Please try. Can't you come up with *something?*

I couldn't help it, he said for the third time.

Stop that, I shouted. Tell me something—one fucking thing about her.

He thought for a moment or looked like he was thinking or wanted me to think he was thinking. Maybe he was giving in or making something up. She smelled like a baby, he finally said.

I told him that smelling like a baby was artificial, fake, no grown woman smells like a baby on her own, and I bet her tits weren't real either or her ass for that matter and how dim was he and how gullible and what was I going to do without my daughter and without her father—what did he expect the two of us to become now?

Friends, he said.

Friends? I was horrified.

Yes, he said.

I don't think so, I said. I'm no friend of yours.

We were quiet then for several moments until he finally said, We haven't been friends in years.

And that hurt me, of course, because I thought we had at least been that.

· · ·

26

I think of that synthetic girl and see her backstage before the show, standing with one foot up on a chair, spreading milky lotion over her legs, using baby powder everywhere, the fog of it clouding around her. Perhaps she's chatting with the others or just being quiet, perhaps she's thinking to herself: *he's out there again, that Robert guy, the weird one who's really into me.*

Robert has been living in a studio across town for nearly six weeks when the woman who calls herself Spruce Love moves into the old tree across the street from our building. She brings a platform, a tarp, a cell phone, and a bucket. She brings blankets, a radio, and protective clothing. I don't actually see her move in, if you can call it that, but when I come home from my Friday night at The Body Shop, there she is in a bright red raincoat and a hat to match, halfway up the tree. It's June now and there's wind but no rain, not a dark cloud above us, and I think about her coat and hat and wonder just who she left on the ground.

The press is here too with their cameras and vans, men and women standing under artificial light with microphones at their chins. My neighbors are out, huddled in small, gossipy groups. Ethel, who lives just below us on the eighth floor, my one and only confidante these days, clutches her robe at the neck and gestures for me to join her.

I sit down on the stoop next to her. Now *this*, I say.

Where you been, Megan? she wants to know.

The Body Shop.

That strip club? Eyes big, she's whispering now, leaning in. Yeah.

Isn't that where Robert had his little problem?

His little problem, yes, I say.

She pats my knee like the grandmother she is.

I had questions. I wanted to talk to someone who was there. I wanted it described to me.

And?

The bouncer tried to be helpful. A nice guy. Friendly.

Interesting, she says.

He sat with me and tried to fill me in.

Really? She raises her eyebrows. Those bouncers are big men, aren't they?

Usually, I say.

And this one?

He's a big man, I tell Ethel, who is smiling and winking. Don't be crazy, I say.

I'm sorry, she says, Robert demanded too much of you— all that sex stuff.

Shhh, I say, looking around at the neighbors, who are thankfully uninterested in us, transfixed instead by what's happening on their street.

It wasn't right he quit his job to mope around the house either, she continues. And he should have picked himself up and went looking for Tessa. He should have been a man, a father, she says, instead of always thinking about his—

She doesn't want to be found, I say, interrupting her.

He should have—

Stop it, Ethel—he's still my husband. We're living separately, that's all. It's not over. We're still married.

Ethel shakes her head. He left you, she says.

It was my idea, I say.

Good idea, she says.

The Millers, who I've never seen, not once, without their three small children strapped to some part of their bodies— his chest, her back, the three-year-old on a leash—stand under the streetlight next to us, alone and unencumbered. Mr. Miller points up at Spruce Love. She's insane, he tells his wife, loud enough for everyone to hear. You're interfering with progress, he hollers, which inspires sneers and shouts from the supporters. They hold their placards high, slap at the wind with their signs. They glare at the Millers, and when they do, I notice Mr. Miller moving toward his wife and taking her hand.

Whose side are you on? Ethel says.

My own, I say.

What about this tree thing? Do the acorns bother you? I remember you complaining about them, she says. Or maybe that was Betty down the hall. She cocks her head, thinking.

Betty down the hall, I say.

I remember now, she says. Betty bitched and bitched. Funny I forgot. I'm getting old, she says, wearily.

You're not, I say.

The years don't lie. She pauses. What do you think about the tree? she wants to know.

It's beautiful, sure, I say, but I've got problems worse than the city tearing it down.

29

Ethel sighs. Have you heard from Tessa? she asks.

Nothing.

I'm sorry, she says.

She'll call when she's better.

Ethel shakes her head. Such a lovely girl, your daughter, she says, such a fine, young—but she's interrupted, and I'm grateful to the van pulling up to the curb, for the smell of exhaust, for the heat emanating from the van itself. There's a loud whoosh, the door opening, and then a dozen or more people spilling onto the street. They circle the tree, hold hands, and begin singing a song I don't recognize. It sounds religious, though, and I wonder how I'll survive the night and if I'll get any sleep at all.

Look, Ethel, I say, more crazies.

They just believe in something is all, she tells me. Don't be—she says, and then stops herself.

What? I say.

Nothing, she says. You've got enough going on, she says.

I was there at The Body Shop because Robert was there, some three nights a week, flaunting our credit card, nodding at the black-haired bouncer, who earlier called me *Cute Eyes* and ushered me to the front of the line with a curling finger and a wink—a gesture I appreciated. It was a long line, one that swirled into the alley like an S—a bold or compliant woman scattered here and there, but mostly it was a line of men, all hats and jackets, shiny shoes and lit cigarettes, all saliva and expectation.

The place was smaller than I imagined; in my mind it was a warehouse, vast and imposing, with tall silver walls, taking up half a block, but the building was a little brown box, insignificant, petty, and sat on the corner of 38th and Triumph Avenue in a part of downtown so down I didn't even know it was there. A sign hung just above the front door that read THE BODY SHOP in black, bold letters, but if you looked closely, you could see that the word STEW had been there first, the letters faint and soft gray, creating a shadow behind the club's newer name. I wondered about that, who would name a place STEW, as I was smiling up the bouncer, mouthing *thank you,* and moving into the club.

Inside, too, was not what I'd expected. One small room and a rickety stage. If they let a big girl dance up there, I was thinking, if she so much as stomped her thick leg one time too many, she would have literally brought down the house. There were two poles for the tandem performance Robert told me about, and the '70s disco ball he described hanging from a wire in the middle of the stage.

When the bouncer had a break, he came looking for me. He sat down, slipping his overgrown body into the little chair with surprising ease. I decided he was my best bet, that if I handled him correctly, he'd give me the information I needed. I turned from him, reached into my bag for my wallet, and let it flip open in my palm. I used my chin to gesture at my husband's face. You've seen him in here, right? I said.

And the bouncer smirked, shook his head. Caveman, he said, laughing. He won't be coming in here anymore, he said.

I know, I said, lifting my screwdriver and taking a big drink. I licked my lips and tasted the orange juice there. I became conscious of my tongue and quickly pulled it back inside my mouth. Caveman's my husband, I said.

He looked at me, at my lips, and said, We've had other guys get crazy. They touch the girls. One guy dropped his pants, like anyone here was paying to see *his* stuff, you know?

I smiled.

But Caveman was different, he continued. We've never had a guy carry a girl off the stage. He picked her up. Just what was he *thinking*?

I thought maybe you'd tell me, I said.

Don't know much about what they're thinking, he said. Just care about how they behave when they're here.

You're a man. You think things, don't you? I said.

Damn straight, he said, smiling, flirting.

I was embarrassed and wasn't sure I wanted the conversation to go that way. I straightened my skirt and decided that if I ever came back here I'd wear jeans. What else did Robert do when he was here? I mean, before that last night. Was there any indication—I began, and then stopped myself.

The bouncer looked at me blankly. No, he said.

No hints, nothing? I pushed.

He thought for a moment, pulled on his short goatee. He squinted, and I thought he might change his mind and open up. Not really, he said.

I picked up my drink and finished it off. A waitress caught my eye, and I lifted the empty glass in the air at her.

Bobby was a big tipper, a good guy, the bouncer said.

He doesn't have a job, I said, immediately regretting giving him that.

He said he had a job. Said he was in sales.

Yeah, well, I said. He used to be in sales.

The bouncer looked around the club, and then at me. You're not young, but you're pretty, he said. What's your name?

Megan, I said. And thank you, I guess.

It's a compliment. You look like you know some things.

I don't know anything. That's why I'm here, I told him.

I wish I could help you out.

What time does the show start?

Next girl goes on at ten.

I was about to ask about my husband's stripper, Scarlet, when the waitress arrived with my drink and a shot of vodka on the side. She pointed at a group of men in the back and told me they were taking care of my tab.

See, the bouncer said, you're pretty. Isn't she pretty, Bev?

She's pretty, Bev said. Are you flirting with the customers? She nudged his shoulder with her tray, teasing.

Maybe, he said.

Bev turned to me. The guys said to drink as much as you want. They'll even pay for your cab home.

I won't be taking a cab.

I'll let them know, she said.

I'm sure Bev was at least twenty-one, but she looked sixteen, the age Tessa was the first time she ran away. I wondered if the waitress's mother knew she worked in such a place. I wondered how her mother would react if she could see her girl serving drinks in a place like this—would she support her kid no matter what or would she stand in Bev's way, a shrill wall? I tipped her a five-dollar bill, mostly because I didn't want the bouncer to think we were poor, and said thank you.

Name's Tweet, the bouncer said, putting his hand out for me.

How'd you get a name like Tweet? I said, taking his hand, shaking it, giving in. I wanted information from him and maybe I wanted attention too. I was shaking his hand, consciously exuding a charm I hadn't used on strangers in years, and it surprised me the way it came so easily to the surface, and I held Tweet's hand that extra fraction of a second, my own hand dwarfed and lost there, and felt my whole body lighting up with the flirtation.

I like birds, he said.

To watch or keep as pets?

Both.

What kind of birds?

I've got a finch, four budgies, and two Amazons, he said.

I looked down at his hand and noticed the ring. What does your wife say? I said.

More to them than to me, he said.

I'm sorry, I said.

She's in real estate. They're her birds really, but I've fallen for them pretty hard. Hey listen, he said, you still married to Caveman?

Yes, I said.

Damn, he said.

We've got an open thing, I lied.

Oh yeah?

I found out from Tweet, whose real name was Jackson, which certainly made more sense, that Scarlet stopped working at The Body Shop soon after the incident with my husband, that sure the money was good, but she'd had enough, the guys were getting weirder by the minute, and she was going back to teaching third grade. She'd just have to make do with less or get her fat husband off the couch and back to work. I found out from Tweet that Robert came in on Mondays, Wednesdays, and Thursdays—those nights I was teaching the Cambodian adults English, their very first words—*hello, nice to meet you, what is your name, my name is blank*—my husband was at The Body Shop, and very generous, apparently, buying drinks for other men.

What men? I wanted to know.

I don't know, he said.

Random men? Anybody?

Pretty much, he said.

I thought of those men, drinking the money I was earning for the three of us, and looked around the club. They were there now, in clusters, in lively groups, one man alone in a corner with a bottle at his lips, a circle of Scandinavian tourists speaking in clipped accents to my left, and in the very back a blur of men asserting their presence with booming laughs.

It wasn't the going there and watching those women, or even his embarrassing generosity that had me chewing my nails and picking at my cuticles for the first time since puberty, but the act that got him thrown out of the place and the feelings that led up to the act.

It went on for weeks, him sitting there, a short drink of dark rum in front of him, a short straw, his fingers and lips around that straw, his eyes, even as he sipped the drink, on her, this third-grade teacher, this Scarlet. He said it was love, not sex or the desire for it, that made him rise from the booth and climb the five stairs to the stage. For several seconds my husband stood in front of Scarlet, using his own body—arms and legs spread out, my husband was an X—to hide her nearly naked one from the rest of the men.

I've been told that some men laughed and hooted, some men whistled, and some men booed and tossed their rolled-up napkins toward the stage, but no man rose to stop my husband, so he picked her up and despite her protests—her yelps, her saying *Fuck, Robert, put me down*—despite her slapping at the air and at his back, he tossed her over his shoulder like a caveman. Hence the nickname.

Robert carried that slim and half-naked girl down those five steps and sat her down in the chair across from his booth. He looked at her. He knelt. He wept into her tasseled breasts for nearly two minutes before she pushed him away.

Where was Tweet when all of this was happening? I asked him now, and he told me about that thin cot in the office in the back of the club, how that afternoon he'd had his wisdom teeth pulled, all four at once, how much it hurt. Even now, six weeks later, the memory of it sent his palm to his jaw. Why'd God give me those four teeth if I didn't need them? he asked.

I smiled at him.

Who's that? Tweet said, looking at my open wallet on the table in front of us.

Our daughter, Tessa, I said. I snatched the wallet up and tossed it in my bag.

What is she, five, six? he said.

That's an old picture. She was six, I said. She's twelve now, I lied.

Good kid? he wanted to know.

The best kid, I said.

I read in Saturday's paper that the oak is three hundred years old. That it's winter deciduous, broad leafed, and the acorns that Betty down the hall hate develop from the ovary of a single female flower. That the tree is fifteen feet across and more than eighteen stories high. That before Spruce Love became a tree sitter, she worked with troubled youth. Some of the kids she helped are out there now with signs, cheering her on. She's a divorced vegetarian and the mother of three boys.

Our condominium is on the ninth floor, and from the bedroom window I can see Spruce Love's platform, two pillows, a gray blanket, a bucket and radio, and what looks like a propane stove, and in the early morning when the press is gone and the believers are comfortable in their own homes, I watch Spruce Love sleep. I sit up, pillows behind my back, in what had been our bed and what is now just mine.

·   ·   ·

Why didn't the other men save her from you? I asked my husband a week before he moved out. It wasn't the question he expected. I'm a regular, he said flatly. Scarlet and I are friendly—she spends her breaks with me.

Wonderful, I said.

It's friendly—we're friendly, he repeated.

Please.

Everyone there knows that we're friends—you might call it something else, but it's friendship—or it *was* friendship.

What's it now, Robert?

It's nothing now, he said.

Well, your good buddy, *your pal* didn't want to be taken off the stage like that, I said. What about the rules? Don't they have rules?

They have rules, Megan. It's a little club. It's not like the big ones. Sometimes they bend the rules, he told me.

I don't understand why no one saved her from you.

Who knows? They were stunned. Maybe they thought I was part of the act.

Nice. Lovely.

We could try therapy, he said.

Tessa's been in therapy—what's it done for her? I said.

She'll be fine, he said.

I shook my head.

You'll see, he continued. She'll wake up one day and take a look around. She'll reach for the phone and it won't be there. She'll go to that outhouse in the winter and it will all be too much. One morning she'll see his wrinkled face, he told me.

Who knows what she sees when she sees him, I said. Who knows what she's looking for?

We sat there for several minutes, quiet, and I imagined my daughter sitting on a hard chair, in a circle of people just as sick as she was, people who missed that drink or needle as much as she did, and I imagined her old man boyfriend sitting next to her, leaning in and whispering in her ear, promising an adventure, and I thought about the two of them on the road, running away from health or us, how ridiculous they must have looked together stopping for breakfast, what the servers and other diners said behind their backs, and I imagined Scarlet too, dancing onstage, smelling like a powdered baby, and I imagined my husband moved by such a scent, and finally I said, Maybe you should try therapy on your own, Robert.

They've given Spruce Love three days to vacate the tree or they're bringing in a crane and forcing her down. She's been up there for several months now and her hair has grown wild, big blond curls sprouting from her head, and her body is smaller—even from here, I can tell. She looks like a little tree herself, crazy branches and leaves atop a thin trunk. If she *were* a tree, I'm thinking, she'd be a palm. The supporters, who disappeared for the last few weeks, are back now and seem to have multiplied in number. Their singing is loud and hypnotic and goes on all the time. I sit at the window and drink my tea and count the hours she has left.

• • •

The night before my husband moved out I couldn't sleep and didn't want him to do so either. I was sitting up in bed in the dark, thinking about our problems. I could hear Robert snoring from the couch and each loud puff made me more and more angry.

When he said that he hadn't, in all our years of marriage, with the exception of Scarlet, touched another woman *that way*, I believed him. When he said he needed time off from his job to deal with Tessa's addictions and his own, I believed him too.

I took that extra job teaching English as a second language at night. During the day I continued teaching at the high school, and then I'd come home and make us a quick dinner before running out the door to the adult education building down the street from our house. I was optimistic, naïve, telling myself that Robert was working through Tessa's problems and his own for the both of us, that when he recovered and stood up, he'd be able to lift me up too.

I went to the couch and shook his shoulder. He groaned and mumbled something. I shook him again. Wake up, I said. There are things I need to say before you go.

Now? he said.

Yes.

What time is it?

Never mind, I said.

He sighed, giving in.

It's not the going there that has me upset—you know that, Robert, don't you?

40

Not really, he said.

I buy the magazines for you myself, I insisted. I stand at the counter and hand over *Jugs* and *Hustler*. I even bought those little balls for you to stick in your ass.

I didn't like those balls, he said, wincing.

But I bought them when you thought you might, didn't I?

Yes, he said.

And I tried watching those silly movies with you. Remember last December? That woman who had sex with a branch?

It wasn't a branch.

It sure looked like a branch—it had leaves. It was ridiculous, I said.

There are better films, he said.

Look, Robert, I've done my best here. I'm tired. I miss my daughter. I'm asking you to leave because I can't take any more, I told him.

I'm leaving. You told me to go and I'm going, he said. What else do you want me to do?

I want you to tell me what's wrong, I said. Tell me what's wrong with both of us. What's wrong with our girl too.

Tessa's coming home, I told you. I know it in my heart. And all men have secrets, he said. I'm not alone in that. I'm not the only one.

Okay, I said, but a man with secrets, maybe he gets up only to shout or hoot, but he doesn't carry some poor girl off the stage. Even a man with secrets doesn't pick a girl up, throw her over his shoulder, and carry her away.

But maybe he wants to, my husband said.

It doesn't matter what he wants, it matters what he does. Let me sleep, Megan. I need some sleep. I've still got packing to do. Please let me—but before he could finish the sentence, I was up, off the couch, and walking back to the bedroom.

There are scenes I imagine. I imagine, for instance, that Spruce Love comes down from the tree on her own, that she's hungry up there and cold, that now the rains have come and her red coat and hat do little to protect her, that she knows this and loves her three sons enough to return to the ground. I imagine too that we come together again as a family, that we sit and eat our toast in peace and relative calm, and by late August we're spending nights on the balcony, Robert and I, looking at our new view of the mountains now that the oak is gone. We sip tea or soda so as not to tempt our newly sober girl if she should join us. We listen for the sound of the screen door shutting, which means she's on her way, moving toward us, and we hear those pink slippers I've begged her to toss out slapping against the soles of her feet, and she pulls up a chair, *Hey Moms, hey Pops,* and sits down with us around the little table. *Damn, he was old,* she says. *What was I doing there?* she asks us.

And then there are facts: that I meet Tweet several times a month in a motel room, that I meet him after my night class, that I say good-bye to my students and head to the designated spot, that I drink the expensive vodka I've asked him to bring, that Tweet is bare-chested in his boxers, leaning down, one hand inside the mini-refrigerator, searching for a snack.

His chest is smooth and dark and lovely.

He smells like musk and birdseed.

He talks to me about the houses his wife sells and the pets he keeps in cages.

Tweet carries the ice bucket and tongs over to the bed, where I'm sitting, waiting for him, in only my slip and bra.

He wanted to be a police officer, he tells me, but couldn't pass the test. I'm dyslexic, he says, standing over me. It's discrimination, he says.

I try to look sympathetic, and think about taking off my bra, but decide instead to wait until he reaches for me.

Is Robert home tonight *looking for work?* Tweet mocks.

Where? I say, nearly forgetting the string of lies I've told this man. That Tessa's twelve years old now, in the eighth grade, first in her class. That she's involved in ballet and mathematics, loves geometry, those angles, those curves and circles. That Robert and I are working things out.

Is he home tonight? he says again.

Not tonight, no, I say.

Where is he? Tweet uses the tongs to drop a pair of ice cubes in my glass.

He's at a meeting, I say.

AA?

No.

What then?

It's sort of a sex addiction meeting, I say—another lie I've got to file away and remember.

Tweet laughs. Not a bad addiction to have, he says. I mean, if you've got to pick one.

Well . . .

43

Maybe we're addicted too, Megan.

I drink once a week, tops, I say.

Not that, *this,* he says, looking around the motel room. He sits down on the bed next to me—strong thigh next to my own that shrinks and pales beside it. We're not in love, right? I mean, we like each other, it's obvious, but we're not *in love.* And we've got people at home that we *do* love.

Okay.

And still, we're here, together, doing this, he says. They're not perfect people, not Stephanie and not your Caveman, but they're ours. We hooked up with them for a reason—or plenty of reasons. He puts the ice bucket on the floor, then leans back on the bed, both arms stretched out behind him.

I guess so.

I'm just saying, he says.

I understand what you're saying, I know what you're saying, I tell him—but of course I don't know at all. I don't know where I'll be in a year from now. I don't know if my daughter is ever coming home. I don't know if I want my husband back. I don't know why I painted my toenails earlier when I haven't done so in years.

Tweet looks happy, like we're in agreement, meeting here, doing this, having cocktails and taking off our clothes.

It would be great to have some juice with this, I tell him. I wish I had some juice, I say.

He picks up the remote and turns on the TV. One sec, he says, flipping channels, I want to see who won the game. He stops at a news channel and there's Spruce Love and the believers. Check her out, Megan, he says. Have you heard about this whacko that's shacked up in the redwood?

It's an oak, I say.

Redwood, oak—what's the difference?

There's a difference, Tweet.

Anyway, check her out. Have you heard about this whacko? he asks again.

I've heard about her, yes, I say. She's not a whacko, I say, she's a believer.

She's a whacko, he insists.

I look into my glass and give Tweet a pleading look. I gently nudge him with my shoulder. I wish I had some juice, orange or grapefruit, even cranberry would be nice, I tell him.

Tweet jumps from the bed and stands up. Okay, okay, I'll go, he says, but you keep watching this. They've given her twenty-four hours and then they're bringing in the crane, he tells me.

I want to say: Tweet, I can see her from my bedroom window and sometimes she's awake at a ridiculous hour, three or four a.m. and I peer at her, part the blinds and stare, and the stars are behind her, and the moon, and all that black air.

I want to say, I watch her read a book or eat her vegan soup by flashlight.

I want to say, Listen, I haven't told you one true thing.

Let me know if she comes down from there, he says. Let me know who won the game.

Liquor store's around the corner, Tweet. Do you know which one I'm talking about?

And Tweet is nodding, stepping into his jeans. The zipper's down, the blue fabric flapped out on either side until he holds the pieces together and zips himself up. I might not be in love with you yet, Megan, he says, but I like you a lot. I hope what I said before wasn't insulting.

I'm not insulted, I say.

Because that's not the kind of guy I am. I wouldn't want to hurt you.

I'm not hurt, I say.

He's nodding but doesn't believe me, I can tell. Maybe it's physical now, what's between us, he says. But who knows what the future holds. Things change, you know what I'm saying? He looks at me, a hopeful, dopey look on his face. Tell me what you want, Megan.

I'm not sure what he's talking about.

The juice, he says. What's your favorite kind?

Oh, I say. Cranberry, I answer.

I like you a lot, Megan, I do. Things change and they might just change for us. I'll go now, he says. I'll get you what you need.

Animals

IN ADDITION TO THIS HORRIBLE HEAT WAVE AND THE trouble with my wife, Michelle, I'm worried about the animals dying at my zoo. Even these 100-degree nights don't explain it. It's been going on too long, for too many years, the dying. My job's to keep the animals alive and healthy. People are beginning to look at me funny, folks I work with. I'm head vet, which is something, considering my parents were butchers. Good people, my mom and dad, but ones who'd pet you at dawn, who'd coo and call you by a nickname, Lover Girl or Chester or Babe, and by dusk they'd crack your neck and have you bubbling in a pot with potatoes and carrots.

I've been at the Los Angeles Zoo for over ten years, and for the last nine the animals have been going at a frighteningly higher rate than the national average. Freak things, accidents we can't explain. Marabou stork chicks, four of them, dying from maternal neglect. She left them, bald and shaking, in the nest. I wanted to say, "Look, they're yours, all of them." I wanted to say, "They're *you*, only fragile and with more needs." In 1992, during the riots, our civil unrest, a gazelle was kicked to death by an ostrich. Two years later, six black-necked swans ate poisonous loquat seeds. The list goes on. Just yesterday my favorite rhino, a huge and beautiful black creature, dropped dead after eating a square of plywood. How can even the best vet help a rhino like that?

That's what I'm thinking about, the animals at my zoo, my job, when Michelle starts in.

"You don't believe her," she says.

"I believe that *you* believe her," I say.

It's after dinner, and the whole house, each and every room—I've been pacing—smells like the garlic I peeled and chopped earlier. I chopped it so fine for so long, chopping and chopping, barely missing my fingers, that when Michelle nuzzled my neck and looked over my shoulder at the pungent mound I was scooting from the cutting board to frying pan, she commented on my ambition, my precision, how horny I make her, even now, twelve years into it. She loves me, she wanted me to know, no matter how much fighting we do these days.

We're side by side on the couch, and Michelle's got her bare feet up on the coffee table. They're the prettiest feet you'd ever see, clean and pale, pink toes with just a hint of curl—she's sweet as a baby, and sometimes I think she's just as new. She's balancing a bowl of ice cream on her hard belly, holding the bowl with one hand. She wears my plaid boxer shorts and a white T-shirt. The ice cream is mint, her favorite, and she's stirring, waiting as she always waits, for the chocolate slivers to melt.

"Stop grimacing, Parker," she says.

"What? Oh . . ." I say.

"It's *my* baby sister who spent the night in jail. I should be the one on edge." She looks at me. "Relax," she says.

"Yeah, yeah," I say, trying to, but it's a hard thing to do, like thinking about *not* thinking about something—a noun, a shoe or ankle, my rhino—then trying to erase the image from my mind. And now, trying to calm down, I'm aware of the veins in my neck, the blood working its way through. "You know I hate it when things get messy," I say.

She looks down at the bowl. "Ice cream's got to be soft, that's how I like it."

"You know what I'm talking about." I sigh and lean back.

"No, I don't know."

"You *should* know."

"Know what, Parker, that she's a liar? She might be a thief, but she's no liar."

"What do you think stealing is?"

"It's not a lie."

"Of course it's a lie."

"She wouldn't lie to me."

"Maybe she would."

"She's my baby sister."

"I know who she is."

"No, you don't. You know about your dead rhino, you

49

know about your stray cats, you know the difference between two gazelles, but about my baby sister—"

"She's been here two months, living under our roof," I interrupt. "She's eaten meals with us. She sits at the table and we feed her," I say.

"You don't know her, what's inside." And my wife is patting her chest with a flat palm. "Not the way a big sister knows a little sister," she says, emphatically.

Sometimes I see a pair of women, strangers, women I've never met—they might be on a bus or in the car next to me, stopped at a red light, the driver putting on lipstick, then turning, smacking her painted lips for her friend's approval, they might be laughing together or talking intently, leaning toward each other at a bar, because whatever they have to say, whatever's causing them to laugh, requires closeness, proximity, and I'll be upset. I'll feel—and this might not make sense—but I'll feel rejected and ignored, left out of something important, another pair of women who won't let me in. Then I'm sad, not just about those women, those two strangers, but about Michelle, my own wife, the place inside her I can't penetrate, about my mother and sister when they're standing in a kitchen or sitting at a table. There's a space between them where I can't go, and even if they said—which they have—*Pull up a chair, Parker, join us,* that space between them, that awesome space, disappears as soon as I sit down.

•   •   •

Michelle's given me reasons not to trust her. Years ago, before she loved me, she gave me crabs. On our second date she listed her former lovers by height and occupation, unable to remember names, and just recently she's admitted crushes on famous men that could sway her away from me, even now, at least for a night, actors and singers and politicians she'll never meet. Tonight, if given the opportunity, she'd throw it all away, open her mouth and legs for Adam Sandler or Shaquille O'Neal or Conan O'Brien. Her taste is eclectic, she wants me to know, and her admissions are about honesty. Can't I see that? Don't I understand? She doesn't tell lies, and neither does her little sister. Michelle wants me to believe the girl is telling the truth.

"I believe that you believe her," I say again.

"That's not enough," she says.

"Look," I say, "I'm just not sure your stepfather's all bad and she's all good. I think Mona has proven how good she is. Shoplifting—that's stealing. She takes things and doesn't pay for them."

Michelle shakes her head.

"No one in my family ever did such a thing, that's all I know." I'm scratching my face, clawing until it occurs to me I could break right through the skin.

"You're all red," she says. "Leave your face alone. You need to shave, Park. Why don't you go inside and pick up a razor, huh?"

She's got a point. Growing a beard in this heat doesn't make sense, and I've been told by more than one person, my brother and a vet at work, Karen, that a beard on me is bad news. It

makes me look tired, weathered, like someone's grandfather—
that's what my brother said. I'm forty-two years old and there's
not a gray hair on my head—it's as black and thick as it was
when I was twenty, but the beard grows in gray and white, more
than giving me away.

People at the zoo, strangers, offer their opinions about my
face. Last week I'm almost certain that an attractive woman in
her thirties grimaced at my beard when I came in to check the
red apes for mites and hydration. I hadn't touched them yet,
the apes. I hadn't done a thing, and there she was, making that
face.

In this heat we give the animals extra water. We point their
bodies toward the shade. We lead the way behind man-made
rocks, steer them into fake caves. And still they drop. On Monday a sable antelope, perfectly hydrated, well fed, got entangled
in an electric fence.

"Curiosity kills them every time," Karen said, matter-of-
factly. We were standing in the hall. It was the end of the day
and Karen was pulling pins out of her hair. With each pin
another red strand fell across her chubby shoulders.

"We've got to be doing something wrong here," I said.

"No," she said, "it's bad luck and nature, curiosity and fear.
Even that marabou stork that ignored her chicks, remember
her?"

"Of course I remember."

"Why do you think that happened?"

"Nature, like you said. Bad luck."

"That's right."

ANIMALS

I wanted to weep suddenly, but stopped myself.

"Things okay with you and Michelle?" she wanted to know.

"Yes," I said.

"Parker, listen, that stork was curious about the new male I introduced her to and afraid the chicks would fuck things up for her. It's sort of like a desperate divorced mom who chooses some jerk over her kids." Karen raised her eyebrows and smiled. "See?" she said.

"No," I said. "We've got to take responsibility. It's not happening elsewhere—not in San Diego or Monterey, not in New York or Florida. My God, I'm supposed to protect them."

"You, my friend, are supposed to cure them when you can, to make them better if, and only *if,* it's possible. You're not a policeman. Or a shrink."

"You're right."

"I saw this woman on television last night. She claimed she was a cat shrink and was yammering on about how lots of cats need Prozac—that all that sleeping and keeping to themselves is really cat depression. Personally, I thought *she* was the one who was nuts."

"What?" I said.

"Forget it, Park. The bottom line is you can't protect these animals from who they are. You understand?"

"I hear you."

"There's nothing you can do about the way they were made." She patted my back. "You're a good doctor," she said.

· · ·

53

In this heat, people are dying too. Thirty in Texas, some half a dozen in and around Los Angeles. Air conditioners break down or people can't afford them. Elderly people literally can't breathe, suffocating in their recliners, feet up, ankles swollen like my rhino's, makeshift fans fashioned out of newspapers, magazines, covers ripped off paperbacks found in their laps. Michelle and I live on the California coast, in Venice, and sometimes the nights and days are so cool we're forced to wear sweaters in the house. It makes me feel grateful and guilty at once, wearing a sweater, when people are dropping dead in their favorite chairs.

There are times I catch myself looking at Michelle's sister Mona. She'll be watering the ferns and palms in the den, bending over in the smallest of shorts, and she's my sister-in-law, yes, but she's also a half-naked girl doing chores.

Once I saw her from our bedroom mirror, her image reflected from the hall mirror into our room. She was swaying back and forth, seductively moving her shoulders and bending at the waist. I wasn't sure whether she knew I was watching or not, but I think she did know, or maybe I just told myself that—wanted to believe the dance was for me. Michelle was in bed, asleep. I had a hand in my wife's soft hair, and outside the bedroom her sister was moving in her nightgown. It was after midnight and the girl was swooning and dancing, her hips to the right, then left, her breasts high and firm under the blue silk gown.

These days, before sleep, I make mental notes. I make lists. I reassure myself about who I am, even though Michelle has told me more than once that a person can't define himself, that whatever it is he says about himself is probably inaccurate. A friend might say, "I'm overly generous—sometimes I just have to control this urge to give," and Michelle raises her eyebrows. A chatterbox claims, "I'm a listener. I don't like to talk." Michelle moans so that only I can hear.

Still, before sleep, I make my list. I tell myself: I am a man who finds stray cats and brings them home. I feed them, then carry them through the neighborhood in my arms, sometimes finding them a place to sleep, a family. I am a man who doesn't cheat on his wife. I am a man who rarely uses the word *fuck* or words like it. I am a man who chops garlic for his wife so fine, risking his own skin. I am a man who, in twelve years of marriage, hasn't as much as flirted with a waitress. I am a man thinking about a fourteen-year-old girl.

Michelle's mother is a good mother in most ways. A drinker, yes, but a decent woman all the same. She accused Mona of trying to seduce her new husband, Big Mac, the banker. That's the word she used—*seduce*. Michelle told me about their phone conversation. "Imagine that," Michelle said, "a girl, a thirteen-year-old child, seducing a grown man."

"Hmm," I said.

"*Hmm*? What the hell does that mean?" she mocked.

"Just what I said—hmm."

55

Michelle insisted on the phone with her mother that Mona couldn't have tried such a thing. She told her mother that they have names for men like that, men caught embracing their new stepdaughters in the den. Perverts. Big Mac was a pervert. In addition to being named after a hamburger, two skinny pieces of meat, he was a perverted son-of-a-bitch. She didn't care how much money Big Mac made, how much he gave to charity, how big a house they moved into, he was still worth nothing in her eyes.

"Why'd you have to make fun of the man's name?" I said, looking at her.

She shook her head.

"What's his name have to do with anything?"

"Think about what you're saying, who you're defending," my wife said.

The last time we'd spent any real time with Mona she was nine years old. Michelle's mother had had a problem with one of her kidneys. Michelle went out there to take care of the house while the woman recovered from surgery. I joined her that last weekend, and my mother-in-law was single then, lonely inside. She sat at the table, newly stitched up, minus a kidney, rubbing the neck of an unopened bottle of Jim Beam. "If I could just find someone," she said to Michelle.

"Who are you looking for?" Michelle asked.

"You know," her mother said, "love."

"Oh, *that*," my wife said, smiling, reaching under the table and letting her hand rest on my knee.

56

Mona was nine, with chubby cheeks and braces, shy, her face down, looking at the floor so intently that once she walked into a wall. A nervous girl. I'd see her chewing on a strand of hair or biting her bottom lip, chewing at her skin even with those braces. She'd stutter when we could get her to talk.

Like I said earlier, Michelle didn't love me yet, at least not fully. At my request, we'd been living together for just two months when she gave me crabs. I thought I loved her enough for both of us, that she'd get some of that love on a daily basis and come to appreciate it and return it, despite her doubt. Still, I thought we were monogamous.

I'd spent three days itching, blaming the summer heat, my laundry skills, the diseased crowned cranes I'd been caring for, the yellow bar of soap, even questioning my own hygiene standards, only to find, after a determined inspection involving my crotch and fingernail, the tiny translucent culprit, just one among many. It was evening and I was holding the crab on my index finger, watching it kick. I was on my knees in the middle of the bed, the sheets twisting around me like a tornado. This is how Michelle found me: my boxers down, my ass clenched and facing her, my finger an inch from my face.

"What are you doing?"

"I'm looking at your Goddamn boyfriend," I said, turning, moving knee by knee toward her, balancing on the mattress. I kept my eyes on the crab and carefully stepped off the bed, as if the rest of my life depended on that action. I held the crab up to her, close to her face where she could see.

She looked at the floor, at my boxers in a circle at my feet, then at my pubic hair. I was red where I'd been scratching.

"You made a promise," I said. She was shaking her head no. "Yes, Michelle, you did. Every time you slept with me you were promising some damn thing." I took her hand, opened it—what might have been a gesture of love, an invitation—and turned my index finger over, placing the crab in her palm. "Some boyfriend," I said.

There were questions: who is he, where did you meet him, how many times, in whose sheets, what sort of scum, and finally, how the hell could you? I spit the questions out, one after the other, not letting her answer, while I struggled with my jeans. I was tucking myself in, buttoning myself up, in a rush to leave the house.

"How old is he?" I wanted to know. "Adults don't get crabs—not where I come from, they don't. Lice is for schoolkids. Who the hell have you been playing with? You're twenty-five years old," I said.

I walked out of the bedroom and down the hall. She followed. "Goddamn it, Michelle, how *old* is this guy?" She was behind me, not answering. I turned my head and saw her arm and hand making their way to my shoulder. I jolted away from her. At the front door I turned, looking into her face. "How old?" I said again.

"He's twenty, Parker. I'm sorry," she said.

By midnight I was on the couch with the guest pillow and blanket, with my green bottle of poison and a tiny comb. RID. It was supposed to kill them. I was watching the late news with

58

my T-shirt half up, my boxers at my knees. I was thinking about the future I had planned in my head with Michelle. I poured the poison on my pubic hair and combed it through. It smelled like ammonia and my crotch began to tingle.

Mona had been here only two days, but there were things she wanted her big sister to know right up front. The first time she kissed a boy she sucked him off as well. She was twelve. She'd put off that first kiss, she admitted, left a handful of boys standing with their lips poised, ready to meet hers, left them surprised on the porch or in the street, one lanky boy holding his rusty bike with one hand and her waist with the other as she leaned away from him. She was afraid of it, of herself, and knew, even though she was a virgin, that once she'd opened her mouth she'd have to open her legs.

"Some girls are just like that," Mona told my wife, "even before they begin."

"I don't understand."

"Some girls should never even kiss a boy—it's bad news from day one."

"You're so young, a little girl."

"No, I'm not a *little* anything. Look at this," the girl said, smacking her curvy hip as she spoke.

"What happened with Big Mac?"

"I have enough boys at school. I certainly didn't want that fat shit."

Michelle laughed.

"He's an old, gross man," she said. "I think he's fifty. He's at that age where men start to look like women, like old-girlies."

"Like old *what?*"

"Old-girlies," she repeated. "You know, it's in their faces— a he/she thing. The man inside him is gone."

"*Really?*"

"Yes, really. Look at Parker," Mona continued.

"What do you mean?"

"Parker's got years left, what, about seven or eight?"

"Until what?"

"Until he's fifty and becomes an old-girlie."

"My God, Mona. You're something else."

"It's true, but don't worry—Parker's still got the man inside him."

"Well, good," Michelle said.

When Michelle told me the story, she watched my face carefully. She didn't take her eyes off me as she recounted her sister's words.

"What are you looking at?" I asked.

"I don't know," she said.

The first time Mona was caught shoplifting was at a local grocery store. The owner, Leo, is a good guy, a generous and trusting grocer. He knows us well—we're regulars, Michelle and me. Instead of calling the cops, he called our house, and because Michelle was teaching I went down there alone. When I arrived, Mona was sitting at a table in the back room. She was smoking a cigarette and chewing bubblegum at the same time—a sickening smell. I didn't know how she could do that, smoke and chew, blow huge pink bubbles in between drags.

"Stop that," I said.

"No," she said.

"Look." I leaned toward her, grabbing her arm, "I said, *stop.*"

She wriggled out of my grip. "You're not my father."

"That's right," I said. "Thank God for small favors," I said.

On the way home in the car I asked her if she wanted me to keep it a secret, her stealing a box of cookies even though she had five bucks in her pocket, even though we give her cash on demand.

"You mean, keep it from Michelle? Not tell her, *ever?*" she said, leaning in, the seat belt pulling at her neck. She grabbed at the belt, held it in her hand, and looked at me.

"I'm telling you something," I said. "If you behave, if you treat the grocer and folks like him with respect, I'll keep it to myself."

"You'd do that for me?"

"Yes."

"Fuck," she said.

"Don't say *fuck.* That's another thing—I don't want you cussing when I'm around."

"What else do you want? Is there something else I can do for you, Park?" she said, coyly, smiling.

"My God, no," I said.

"That's cool," she said, letting the seat belt smack against her chest and looking out the window. "Whatever."

I was looking straight ahead at the car's bumper in front of us. I did not look at her. I caught my own eyes in the rearview mirror and quickly looked away.

The second time she got caught was in July. This time they arrested her. They found several sweaters underneath the baggy shirt she was wearing. She forgot to detach the theft protection device on one of the sweaters, and as she walked out of the double glass doors at Macy's the bells and buzzers went off. When Michelle arrived, Mona was sitting next to a fat bald man with a badge, admitting everything.

"It means she's honest," Michelle said the next morning, "that she admitted it, you know?"

"She was caught, Michelle. Cornered."

"Still, she could have made up a story. Lots of kids make up stories to save their hides."

I lifted the coffee cup to my lips, raised my eyebrows.

Michelle bit down on her bagel. "She's a kid," she said, mouth full, chewing and talking at once.

"Yeah," I said.

"Kids do things—lots of them don't get caught, that's all. Every kid snatches something, Parker—bubblegum, toys, small things, Matchbox cars and Barbie dolls."

"And later," I helped her along, "dirty magazines and sweaters."

"Yes," she said. "That's right."

"I didn't do that."

"Maybe you don't remember. Did you ever think that maybe you just forgot?"

"I'd remember."

"Well, you're better than the rest of us, what can I say?"

I took a long sip of my coffee. I thought about my rhino, who was then a vision, healthy and strong, who had recently flown through his physical—shiny coat, good digestive system, everything in working order.

"And my sister," Michelle continued, "perhaps she isn't very good at being a thief. We should be relieved, actually." She was nodding. There were crumbs on her white robe, a spot of red jelly.

"You're making a mess," I said.

She looked down at her robe and shrugged.

"I think you should ask Mona about Big Mac one more time."

Michelle shook her head.

"I think you should find out what happened."

She put the bagel down hard on the little plate. "Look, Parker," she began, but didn't finish.

"The girl's proven that she's not perfect. Kids make mistakes. You said it yourself."

"What's your problem?" she said.

"This isn't about me."

"Maybe it should be, Parker."

"It's about your sister," I insisted.

"It might be about you," she said. "You better figure it out. You better fix *yourself,* that's what I think. Enough with the pandas and rhinos and hippos. Take a good look in the mirror," my wife told me.

"Let me ask you this," I begin now, taking the bowl of ice cream from Michelle's belly and setting it on the coffee table.

"Hey," she says, "I was eating that. It's perfect now, soft and—"

"Shhh," I say. "Listen," I tell her. I'm holding her hands, looking into her face. She is thirty-seven, my lovely wife, with the skin of a woman half her age.

"Maybe no one endured what Mona endured. Did you ever think of that, Dr. Spock?"

"No," I say, "but I thought of this—I thought, hey, gee, you can't always believe a girl her age, sometimes they lie."

"They don't lie about that." Michelle's voice is soft, barely audible. She is looking at the greenish-gray mess on the coffee table. She is thinking about picking up the bowl to spite me, I can tell.

"I thought, hey, gee, maybe he didn't do it, at least not what she said he did. Maybe it didn't happen exactly the way she said it. That's what I'm saying, Michelle, it may be ugly, what I'm saying, but I'm saying it."

"Stop it."

"Let me ask you this," I say, unable to stop, unable to leave my wife alone. I let go of her hands, thinking at least give the woman back her hands. She leans back, away from me. She stretches her arms out wide against the top of the couch. They could be wings, those long arms. She could be a bird, I'm thinking, ready for flight, an eagle or hawk, something beautiful and wild. "Do you believe every single girl in the world who claims she was touched by daddy or stepdaddy or whoever, is always telling the truth?"

"Yes," she says.

"A hundred percent of the time?"

"Yes," she says again.

"No," I say, "even you don't think that."

"Don't tell me what I think."

"Listen, I'm not talking a majority here, I'm talking a tiny number. There's a girl somewhere who's telling a lie, that's all—one girl out of millions maybe, but she's lying. Maybe she's got reasons to hate him, but still she's not telling the truth."

"Stop it, Park. Please," my wife says.

"She's standing somewhere in this world and she's talking to someone, a teacher or girlfriend, and she's spewing lies. He did other things, this man she's lying about, perhaps he kicked the dog or even her mother, maybe her curfew is ridiculous, he did other things, but he didn't do *that*." I lean forward and pick up the remote. I do nothing with it, turn nothing on, but the threat is here in my palm.

"I feel sick," she says finally.

I lean back. I say nothing.

"Really sick," she says.

"I'm sorry," I say, weakly.

We sit in silence, my wife and I, through the nightly news.

A woman in Hancock Heights left her baby girl in a parked car. The temperature went over 120 degrees in that car and the child literally cooked. The mother is young and sloppy, hair in her face and bad teeth. Didn't she know a human being could cook like a piece of meat? She's staring into the camera, saying, "My baby. My baby. I didn't know it was that hot. I didn't think I'd be that long." Michelle shakes her head. She doesn't look at me.

We watch half a sitcom without saying anything. We don't laugh at the funny parts, things that would have normally made us laugh out loud. Once, I think I see her lips twist into what might be a smile, but then, no, she's too mad to give me that. Michelle's just about to drink that gross ice cream of hers, the lip of the bowl in her mouth, when I say, "I'll go shave for you. I'll do that," I tell her.

Tag

JANE IS SITTING IN A MOTEL ROOM WITH HER LEGS HANGING
over the bed. The man who's nearly a stranger sleeps, his face
to the wall. She sees yellow carpet, his shoes under the table,
one white sock, and her own fancy underwear.

Outside, the sun is coming up.

Last night is mostly black now, gone to her, but there are
things she remembers. Like his name. She remembers twisting
on the barstool, facing him, and lifting her eyes. "Jones?"

"Yes," he had said, almost apologetically. "It's a last name, I
know, but it's my first name."

"Nice. I like that. Jones," she said, moving a piece of hair
behind her ear. She was getting to that familiar, liquor-induced
place where suddenly she felt more attractive and sensual,
where sex was imminent, and simple things like a man's first
name teased and interested her. "Jones," she said again.

She remembers, too, their last drink, something short and creamy and sweet. He ordered it without asking her; it was his first assumption, that she liked sweet drinks. She hated them, in fact, but swallowed the frothy things down appreciatively, smiling. She remembers the white freckle of whipped cream on his bottom lip, how his tongue dashed out to get it and quickly went back inside his mouth.

After that drink everything went black, became lost in Jane's head, sat somewhere inside her with other too-drunk evenings and unbearable events from the past. She doesn't remember the two of them, after an hour's search, finally finding a motel, which wasn't fully occupied. And she doesn't remember the vacancy sign, the V gone, leaving the word ACANCY in neon red letters, how she found the word funny, so funny that she laughed out loud, tossed to one side, and hit her head on his car window. "Acancy," she said to him, not even slurring.

Now she rubs her head, wondering what she hit and when.

Jane is most comfortable after shots of tequila, and if it weren't for deadly diseases, would sleep with strangers more often. Unlike most women she knows, evenings with men she's only just met do not frighten her. And mornings are interesting. She likes to watch them drink their coffee—one of them squirming, one of them guilty, twirling the ring on his finger—another proud, beaming with his bad skin or soft belly, lifting his coffee cup high. The ones who invite her to eggs and toast would probably call; it means they can eat and look at her. The ones who curl into corners or leave in the night are more like her. It is nothing she brags about.

Early last night she left her apartment with two condoms in her bag.

She sprayed her neck with perfume at the door.

She took a train to another town.

Jane remembers once, a few years ago, a friend of hers commenting that women are lucky. "The least attractive of you can go out and get sex any time you want," Bruce said, envious.

In bed, Jones flinches in his sleep. That something frightens him makes her want to touch him, but she resists. She has learned some things. About deprivation and seduction—how though only hours earlier he complimented her skin and teeth, her hands and sense of humor, how he placed himself inside of her, how she opened—still, these moments in the new light are unpredictable, and any one of her gestures may be read as desperate, or worse, much worse, as intrusive, like she's crossing some line, entering a territory of real concern where she's not been invited. In her early twenties, if a man like Jones panicked in his sleep, she would have moved toward him, pressed her breasts into his back, and left them there, like that—her breasts against his back while he slept. Instead, she watches him flinch and does not move.

· · ·

Years ago, when Bruce said, "The least attractive of you can go out and get sex any time you want," Jane had the urge to lift the checkered napkin from her lap and cover her face with it. She remembers fighting the urge, lifting instead her wine, taking a big drink. She remembers holding the wine in her mouth for several seconds before swallowing. She remembers letting him talk.

They were just friends, coworkers, out to dinner on payday. His teeth were bad, small and brownish, but the rest of his face was beautiful, bright gray eyes and fine bones. As he uncorked the second bottle of wine, he stared at her in a way that said that he knew what she looked like naked, that he'd imagined her standing before him, and had the image in his mind. She was sure he could recall the image whenever he felt the urge, and he felt the urge now, obviously, staring at her like that, a tricky grin on his face.

He'd never behaved that way before and Jane was surprised. "You didn't get your raise, did you, Bruce?" she asked.

"Nope," he said.

"You're angry?"

"Hell yeah."

"You feel like you deserved it."

"Damn right. Deprived of something that should have been mine. You know it, right? I deserved it—absolutely. Fuck it," he said.

They were at an Italian restaurant downtown, and Bruce was changing the subject or not changing it at all. He was leaning forward, enunciating each word, saying, "Men need sex in a way women don't, Jane. I think friends should be able to have sex, *just sex,* and leave it at that." He lifted his glass in the air and looked at her.

"It's bad for friendship," she said, not knowing exactly what it was she meant, if it was his teeth or bad manners, or the fact that she'd have to see him every day at work. She imagined herself sitting with him at meetings, standing with him at the copy machine, behind him at the water cooler, acting like nothing had happened, and decided that if she had sex with him that night, each workday following—each mundane, previously harmless interaction—would carry in it some small and brutal rejection.

When the second bottle of wine was finished and the pasta was smelling bad, hardening on the plate in front of her, he said, "We should be able to do it. You and me, we should be able to walk out of here, go across the street to my apartment, and fuck." He was looking at her intently. "Let's go. Let's give it a whirl."

"I'm not a carnival ride," she'd said.

"A what?"

"Nothing."

"Don't you want to? I know you want to."

She was saying "No," but inside she was drunk enough to wonder where she stood on his attractiveness continuum. "The least attractive of you . . ." he had said. She wondered what he saw when he looked at her. And she hated herself for giving him that.

"No," she said again.

The smile on his face disappeared. He was scowling, wagging his finger at her like an angry father. "See, you don't need it the way I do. If you needed it, you'd leave with me."

"We're friends," she had said, wondering if they were even that now.

"Women are different," he had said.

At eight in the morning, Jones sings out a yawn and Jane is sitting in a wooden chair by the window, watching twin little boys in the parking lot. They scream and laugh, zigzagging their way from one end of the lot to the other. One boy chases, and the other boy runs from him. Because they are twins and dressed alike, Jane watches closely to see who is chasing whom. She wants to understand the game. It is impossible however; they are identical. Every time she blinks or pauses, she is confused.

One boy crouches behind the huge metal trash bin, hiding. He is panting, curling his body into something small. She can see him perfectly from the window, his small back falling and rising. The other boy runs between parked cars, searching. His mouth hangs open. It is a big job, this search. Within minutes, he finds his twin and slaps the boy's shoulder. Then, the boy whose shoulder was slapped fills with a new energy; he is now *It*.

"Tag," Jane says.

The boys wear matching yellow sweaters and little jeans. They look around seven. Jane is thinking about turning thirty next month and how she's never loved any man enough. "Cute boys," she says to Jones, and then she's suddenly embarrassed, afraid he'll feel pressured by her comment, afraid he'll think she wants him, after just one night, to give *her* cute boys.

He sits up in bed, calls her to him by waving the blankets.

In the sheets Jane opens her mouth and legs. It is here, like this, that she can tell Jones with her hot skin that she likes him. He is moving and she is moving and she is listening to the little boys' high voices. They could almost be girls. One little boy screams "motherfucker" and Jane hears him clearly while the man on top of her takes her ear in his mouth.

"Let's take a shower together," he says, smiling, up on one elbow now, cheek in his palm.

She shakes her head.

"Come on," he says.

"I don't think so," Jane tells him, thinking that showering together is not what she does, that showering together is too much, that she will not stand up naked with a bar of soap in her hand—not with him.

"Why not?"

"It's too much," she says. "It's something you do with someone you know really well."

"What do you think we just did?" he says.

And she tells him that she is not at all sure what she did.

He walks to the bathroom alone, and she sees he is angry—his butt clenched into two fat fists.

•   •   •

Minutes later he stands with a towel around his waist and another around his neck. His chest is wet, drops on the few dark hairs. He looks somewhat recovered.

"The boys are still out there," he says.

"Hmm?"

"The boys you were watching. The cute ones."

"They're not so cute," she says.

"I want to take you to the train station, Jane—want to see you off, get your number. Do you want breakfast? You hungry?" She shakes her head, reaches for her shoe.

"Come here," he says. "Stand here, look at the boys with me."

Jane goes to the window, stands there with Jones, holding her shoe in her hand. She is about to ask him something: his last name, how he feels about the war, if his parents are still alive. Something. She is about to ask him something when the little boys start fighting. There's pushing and more name-calling. There's *Fuckwad* and *Pussy* and *Asshole.* One boy punches the other boy in the face. Hard. His fist flying from his shoulder and landing on the other boy's nose and mouth. And then they are on the ground, rolling around, pulling each other's hair. They are screaming. One boy is crying. Or they both are. And then a father or maybe an uncle stands above the boys, says something Jane cannot make out, and the boys stop fighting. They roll to opposite ends of the man's outstretched arms and then stand up. One boy wipes his nose with the back of his hand. They are panting. Their faces are red. They are fixing their little jeans when Jane turns from the window.

Soup

THE THREE OF THEM SIT AT MY KITCHEN TABLE, WITH THICK arms in white T-shirts, waiting for Willy while I make soup. It's early December and they are my son's new friends. They come from Sparrow Park, six miles from where we live. These are the boys who taunted my Willy five years ago, before high school, before his chest grew broad and voice deepened, the boys who called him *Faggot* and *Pussy* and *Flower.*

One of these boys sat on my son's chest, and blackened his eye and split his bottom lip, while another one held his feet and tied his shoelaces together so that when my boy finally stood, he stumbled forward and fell. And one of these boys was the gleeful lookout who cheered and shouted and cursed my son through the whole ordeal, his eyes darting side to side, doing his job.

These are the boys I'd told William to stay away from, the boys his father told him to ignore.

These are the boys I see lately standing on Almont Avenue, my own son among them, cigarettes hanging from their bold mouths.

These are the boys I've invited into my kitchen.

Though my son is seventeen he's still my baby, and though lately he looks at me with disdain and doesn't listen well, he's still my most important man.

I was telling William that his new friends, those boys, are changing him, that it's all there in the way he smirks and stands, in the way he rips apart his bread, some big change. I hear it in his voice when he tells me to stay out of his business. "I'm just growing up," he says. "Get your own life," he tells me.

I was sitting at one end of the couch with a magazine open in my lap, and Willy, in his black jacket and jeans, was sitting at the other end, as far away from me as possible. It was dusk, a Friday in late September. One of those boys would be calling or pulling up to the curb any minute. Willy looked at his watch, then at the front door. He stared at the phone, willing it to ring, I could tell.

"Those boys were cruel to you. They called you names. You came home crying," I reminded him.

"I was a baby, a stupid kid."

"Your grades were good. You were respectful. You listened when your father had something to say. What would your father say now?"

"Can't say much from where he is."

I shook my head. "That's terrible."

"Yeah, well . . ."

"You used to look me in the eye. What sort of boy can't look his mother in the eye?"

"I'm *not* a baby," he said, emphatically.

"Is that what a baby is, a boy who studies? A boy who loves his mother?" I slapped the magazine closed, then put it down on the coffee table. I stared at him.

"I was *your* baby," he continued. "I was weak."

"They were bullies, those boys—and I'm sure they're bullies now. You came home frightened, torn jeans, a black eye that one time, a bleeding mouth. They beat you," I said.

"It wasn't a beating." He stretched his arms out, knitted his fingers together, and cracked his knuckles.

"Your mouth was bleeding, your face—"

"People change," he interrupted, his voice rising.

"Who changes? You or them?" I wanted to know.

A car pulled up to the curb, the headlights illuminating the front curtains, and then the horn, loud and long, unrelenting. I imagined one boy's big impatient palm weighing down on it.

"I was weak," he repeated, nearly jumping up from the couch, grabbing his keys and wallet from the side table. "I deserved what I got. A baby deserves it." He stuffed the wallet into his back pocket and headed to the door, which he rushed through and slammed on his way out.

Now, though, I am standing in my favorite blue dress with my hair done up, making small talk with the three of them. I am cutting up carrots and onions and celery, pulling apart a chicken, smiling at the boys as if they are gentlemen. I ask them about sports, the games they refuse to play. I ask about their classes, which I know they don't attend, and they tell me what I want to hear, what no one in this kitchen believes. An A on this test, a B on that one, how science lab is terribly interesting, and I find myself playing along, pretending to believe them, the most naïve part of me almost doing so.

One boy—and this surprises even me—I give a special smile, one filled with all the tension I've been missing. His name is Foster, and he is tall, the tallest of the three, well over six feet. His big knees hit the bottom of my table. The table is small and round, and as Foster stretches out his legs and grunts slightly, the huge black boots appear on the other side, near me, and I am thinking: he could touch me with those filthy soles *sitting down*. He is that long.

"Small table," he says.

"Big legs," I say, immediately embarrassed by my inappropriate comment. There is blood in my face; I can feel it.

He grins, eyebrows raised.

"Willy's almost ready to go. He'll be out here in a second," I say nervously, turning back to my pot of water, which has just now begun to boil. I scoot the vegetables into my palm and drop them into the pot. They make a little splash and I jerk backwards, my eyes back on the boy.

He is blond, with a strong face, chiseled; there is nothing soft about him; he is all hard angles: his nose, the bones of his jaw and cheeks. His hair, slicked back into a ponytail, is meant to be dramatic, but it is the eyes that strike me, not only their strange color, but the premature lines forking to his temples when he grins. He claims to be nineteen, but his skin and confidence say otherwise.

This much is clear: he is the leader, the one who tells these boys when to scowl or laugh, what brand to smoke, tells them where they will spend their Friday nights, in whose arms, tells them what to eat, whom to hate, how much their shoulders should swing when they walk. He is the one to whom teachers, mothers, and police address their questions.

"What's your father do?" I ask him.

"Heals people," he says, waving his palms in the air like a man of God.

"Preacher?"

"My dad's a doctor," Foster says. "Cardiologist."

"Oh, the heart," I say. "Nice."

"*Diseases of,*" he says, smiling.

I'm uneasy, wiping my hands on my apron. "Want a glass of milk, some fruit juice?" I ask them.

When I hand the boys their drinks, I notice that what I'd mistaken for a mole between Foster's eyes is really a pimple. The eyes are green and glassy, almost gray; they are even more striking up close. The pimple is dark red, scabbed over, and it sits there in the middle, between those glorious eyes, like a target. I try to look into the eyes, but the pimple demands my attention; I can't take my own eyes from it. But I am like this. I get fixed on something and can't let go.

I am looking at the pimple, saying, "What's your favorite food? Do you like soup, Foster?"

"I like all sorts of stuff. I'm not fussy. What you're doing there looks good, smells good too," he says.

One of the boys laughs and shakes his head. The other one gets up from the table and stands against the wall, hands drumming impatiently on his thighs. He gives us a cranky look.

"Chill out," Foster tells him.

The boy stops drumming. "I wish Will would hurry up, that's all," he says, suddenly meek.

It's rumored that Foster raped a fourteen-year-old girl out by the river, a girl he dated for six months. No one in town blames Foster; they all blame the girl. It's simple, you see a boy for six months, especially a boy like Foster, then you agree to certain things, and if the boy can't stop, if he refuses to stop, then you wipe yourself off and be quiet about it.

"Did he do it?" I asked William.

We were sitting at the dining room table, eating breakfast. It was a Sunday and he'd been sick the last few days, flushed and sweating and temporarily agreeable. I'd brought him tea and oatmeal cookies the night before, which he happily accepted, and while he slept I covered him with an extra blanket. At breakfast he looked better, color in his face, but the smirk and bad attitude had returned. He buttered his toast forcefully, sending black crumbs all over the table.

"What happened with your friend and the girl?" I persisted.

"How should I know? It's not like I was there," he said.

"Did he hurt her?"

"Look, she went out to the river with him." He stabbed one of his eggs with a fork. "He invited her and she went along."

"Did he rape her?"

"He had a ring in his pocket."

"A *what?*"

"A *ring,*" he said, exasperated. "He was going to propose. Would a guy go and rape a girl he planned to marry?" He lifted a bite of egg to his mouth. A drop of yolk sat on his bottom lip. "Does that make sense, Ma?"

"No," I said, "it doesn't."

Later that night, the two of us were in front of the television. Willy sat in his father's recliner, leaning forward, lacing his boots, getting ready for another night out. Every now and then he looked up from his task to stare at the young model on the screen. She was selling lipstick. *It's kiss-proof,* she said, puckering up.

"Why not stay in one night?" I suggested.

He rolled his eyes.

"You're just getting over the flu. I've heard it's a bad one, that there's often a relapse."

"Nothing's wrong with me."

"You used to like to read. You used to like to play Scrabble and gin rummy."

"Jesus."

"There are other things a boy might do on a weeknight, that's all. Productive things."

"Productive, huh?" He looked down, noticing something on his boot, a scuff, a mark I couldn't see. He licked his fingers and tried to rub whatever it was away.

"If your friend raped that girl, you have to stay away from him." My voice was flat. I did not look at my son.

"I told you, he had a ring in his pocket. Shit," he said, getting up, giving his boots one last look.

"William . . ." I began.

And he closed the front door before the question left my lips.

I am thinking about how attractive Foster is, even with the rumor, even with that pimple, when William comes out, freshly showered from the bathroom. He looks at his three friends, then at me. When he's wet like this, hair two shades darker, he looks like his father.

"Why not dry your hair before you leave?"

He ignores me.

"You were sick, Will," I continue. "You're still getting over it. I'm making this soup especially for you, so you can get well."

He glares at me, irritated, then looks back at his friends, resting his eyes on Foster. "I just can't get clean," he says. "No matter how hard I wash, I still smell like the stables, like pure shit."

The boys laugh.

"When were you at the stables? What stables?" I ask him. "There are no stables around here."

"Really," he says, "is that so?"

And the boys laugh even harder.

It's been a long four years since my husband Bill died, and during that time I've not been alone in a room with any man that's not family. I've forgotten what this pull feels like, the way it brings the heat to my skin, the way I'm suddenly younger and lighter, and my voice is a lilting foreign sound coming from my throat.

Foster is a big, manly kid, but I don't plan on touching him. I just want to talk some more, feel attractive. Not that I felt all that attractive when Bill was alive. Mostly he wanted to be alone, quiet in his black chair with the newspaper and a pack of cigarettes in his lap. Mostly he spent time holding one unlit stick between his hairy fingers, remembering. Mostly he preferred the sound of his own sickly breathing to anything I might say.

But it's true that I'm attracted to the boy, true that he's a bully, my son's social boss, true that I'm standing here in my kitchen acting like a flirty girl, and I'm not sure what to make of it, to make of myself being attracted to such a person. It makes me wonder. It makes me stop and look at myself. It makes me not like what I see.

The day the boys split Willy's lip open and tied his shoelaces together, his father did what he could, what little he was capable of. "Some struggles you can't win," his father had said, and he might have been talking about his own, the emphysema that was, by then, having its way with him. "I wish I had some pointers, some advice to give you that might take these boys down." My husband sighed, frowned, admitting his own weakness. He was frail, coughing into a handkerchief he'd pulled from his pocket. He turned to Willy, who was sitting at the kitchen table with a towel at his lip, then turned back, resting his eyes on the television that wasn't on.

"*Bill*," I said.

"What?" He paused. "I've got nothing. I don't know what to tell him. What do you want me to say?"

"*Something*," I said.

"Take another route home," he said.

"Let me call the police." I got up from my chair and went toward the phone in the kitchen, but Willy stopped me, grabbing at my upper arm. "No," he said.

"I'll call the parents then. I'll talk to their mothers—a mother understands."

"You do that, Ma, and I'll never recover."

And I knew. He wasn't talking about the black eye or split lip, the two distinct flaps of flesh that would grow back into one thin, white scar, but something else, what was churning around inside of him. "Okay," I said. "I understand," I told him. "Leave a little early. Go down Green Street and up Fifth," I'd suggested.

William and the two other boys are talking about seeing a movie, one in which a girl is killed in a butcher shop. The movie is called *Meat* and Foster is saying that he already saw it, that he loved it, that he'd rather stay here and eat my soup. He says he wants to stay behind. "I'll hang out here," he says.

William looks nervous, intent, like he's making some big decision. He pulls on his chin, a gesture that reminds me of his father. "No, man, come with us. We'll see a different flick, something you haven't seen."

"He can help me clean up," I say brightly.

"No," my son says, firmer this time.

I wave my hand at the mess, the cutting board, the chicken bones and pieces of yellow skin. "I could use some help."

"Stay out of this. You don't know what you're doing," William says.

"I'm just saying . . ."

"Shut up, Ma."

"Hey," Foster says, standing up. "Don't talk to your mother like that. She's a good woman."

William shrinks, his shoulders drop. He looks at Foster, his hero, his boss. "Come on, man," he says, almost pleading. "Come with us. We'll do something else. We don't need to see a movie."

Foster shakes his head.

"We'll go to the stables," my son says, and there's desperation in his voice now. "Yeah, the stables. You love the stables," he reminds his friend.

"Go ahead," Foster says, his voice serious, unwavering. "I'll see you dudes later," he tells the three of them.

I touch my son's back, and he doesn't recoil, just stands

there with my hand on his shirt. "When the movie's over, you boys come back and eat some soup," I say.

William was fourteen when his father died. After a small funeral and an even smaller gathering in our home, we were alone in the living room with his father's empty chair, with a horrible combination of smells: too many sweet flowers and various casseroles left on the dining room table by well-meaning neighbors.

William sat on the carpet, his back against the living room wall, mumbling to himself. I sat down in Bill's chair and missed him with a fierceness I hadn't imagined.

"Want to talk?" I said finally.

He shook his head.

"They say it's good to talk." I wrung my hands. "Maybe I could talk to you."

"About what?"

"I don't know."

"I don't want to talk," he said. "And I don't want to listen, either."

I sighed. I tried to stay quiet but couldn't stop myself. "Should I throw out Mrs. Crane's casserole? Do you think you'll eat it? There's spinach in that one."

He shrugged.

"They say it's good to talk, Willy," I persisted.

"Who's *they*? The same *they* that tells you what cheese to buy? *They* say it's good. They're all eating it. They love it." He was mimicking me, stepping up and away from the wall then, gesticulating, coming my way.

"Stop it," I said.

"*They* don't know nothing," he continued, his hands still moving, his bare feet going now too. My boy nearly dancing in the dim living room.

"You're hurting me."

"What do you think they know? What can they tell me, Ma?" His face was inches from mine. There were several dark hairs on his chin. He was growing fast, my son, and I thought I could sense him growing out of his shoes, his toes pushing through the leather; I thought I could sense his whole body shooting up and away from me.

"Stop it," I begged.

"You don't know nothing yourself."

I started to whimper.

"And *he* knew even less."

As soon as we hear William's car pull out of the driveway, Foster sits back down at the table and asks if I have any music in the house. I point to the den.

"The tapes and CDs are my husband's."

"*Were,*" he says. "The tapes *were* your husband's."

"Yes, well . . ."

"I don't mean to be rude, Mrs. Dunn, but he's dead, right?"

"Yes," I say softly.

"What's it been two, three years?"

"It's been four."

"Damn," he says, leaning back in the chair, looking me up and down. "What have you been doing for four years? A pretty woman like you."

"I've been taking care of my son," I say, turning back to my soup.

"What about yourself?" he says. "You been taking care of yourself? What about you?" I hear him get up then, hitting his knee hard on the table. "Fuck," he says. "Goddamn it, my knee."

I lift the lid, feel the steam on my face, and breathe in. Chicken and vegetables, carrots and onions and celery. Pepper. Dill. I do not answer the boy; I am thinking instead about my soup.

"Hey," he says.

I turn and look at him.

"You okay?" He is rubbing his knee, waiting for an answer. "How're you doing? You were so friendly before. What's wrong?"

I look at Foster's face, his eyes, his jaw, the pimple. "I don't know," I say.

"You can't just turn a guy on and then turn him off. I'm not a fucking teapot," he says, taking a step toward me.

"The CDs are in the den, go in the den and put one on, I know most people prefer CDs these days, but me, I miss records, I do, I really do—I miss how careful you had to be when you put one on . . ." I am stirring my soup, rambling.

88

He takes another step.

"I don't like those little disks," I continue, my voice breaking, "too little, too easy to misplace. I'm always losing things. I lose my keys, money. Happens all the time. I hate it. I bet you don't lose anything. Put it away, you know exactly where it is. Your belongings, I bet you keep track of them."

"Shhh," he says.

"And I bet you like CDs, being so young—I'm not so young," I remind him. "I could be your mother."

"You've been alone a long time now, right?"

I should not answer the boy, I should stop right here, and not say a word.

"Right?" he repeats.

"I've been alone," I say.

I wanted Willy to be my friend. I wanted us to drink coffee together. It was selfish and unmotherly of me. The boy was fourteen and friendless. His father was dead. He sat in his room with the curtains closed for hours at a time, listening to music I didn't even try to understand. He ate his breakfast in there and his lunch too, sitting at his desk with a plastic tray of food. At dinner, I insisted he sit across from me and it seemed to pain him, lifting the fork to his mouth, such proximity to his lonely mother. I wanted him to drink coffee so he would sit with me in the mornings and discuss things: the neighbors, the news, his grades and dead father. I thought if I could get him to like coffee that maybe he'd start spending time, that together we'd recover. After dinner one night I served him a cup, heavy cream and sugar. "An adult beverage," I said.

He lifted it to his lips and took a sip. He sneered, first into the beverage itself and then at me. "I hate it," he said.

"Don't you want to be an adult?" I said.

Foster's in the den now, putting on Patsy Cline, and I stand in the kitchen doorway, wondering how to get rid of him. I walk out of the kitchen, into the den, where he's standing, moving his slim hips to the music. I take off my apron, roll it up, and hold it in my fist.

"What a voice," he says.

"I think you should leave," I say.

"What?" He gives me a puzzled look; he wants to be nice now.

"I think you should go. I want you to go." My voice is calm, but inside I am bubbling, I am bubbling like my soup.

"But you like me, Mrs. Dunn. I know you do. Things like that don't just disappear."

"Of course they do," I say.

"Oh come on, you're wondering about me, even now, I can tell."

I shake my head.

"You wanted me to stay, remember?"

"I made a mistake."

Foster looks at the couch. "Sit here a minute," he says, almost sweetly, like a baby.

I shake my head.

"Come on," he says. "Just one minute, then I'll go."

"I want you to go *now.*"

"Just one minute," he purrs.

I point to the far end of the couch. "You sit over there," I tell him.

He sits down. I stay standing. "Foster," I say, surprising myself, "why'd you boys let William in? It doesn't make sense to me."

"Huh?"

"Why'd you let him join your group?" And as the question leaves my lips, I'm afraid of it.

He puts his elbows on his knees, holds his face in his hands. "Will changed," he says.

"He's growing up, yes."

"He's not the pussy he once was."

"He wasn't a—"

"I beat her," he says, cutting me off.

"The girl by the river," I say. Calmly. Like I knew it all along. Like I knew it all along and wanted him anyway. Like he is what he is. And my son is what Foster is. And I am what they both are because I allow them to be that way, because I make them soup.

"I wasn't alone," he says.

I say nothing. I do not move.

"People think I was alone, but that's not true," he tells me.

I shake my head. My body tightens and closes.

"I had company," he says.

91

I squeeze my apron.

"I wasn't alone," he repeats, standing up, walking over to me, grabbing my chin with his finger and thumb. I am pushing away from him, but he is pulling me into his chest. "Everyone was there," he says, kissing me, roughly, hard and full of hate, pressing his face on my face, and the pimple between his eyes opens, splits, begins to bleed. He paints my face with his pimple, kissing me, saying, "Let me tell you about your son."

I don't know what that girl was doing out on the river with Foster, I don't know what she was thinking, how much she planned to give away, if a part of her said *yes*, what part said *God no*, what part he wanted to hear, and heard, what part he felt up with four long fingers inside of her. I don't know what noises she made, how small she became, or if she's growing yet. I know this: I have his blood on my face, my forehead, my cheek, I know his scab is somewhere in this carpet, I know the skin is pink and wet and open there like a misplaced eye, I know I must wipe myself off, and stand by the window, and hold the curtain, and listen, and listen for my boy. I know soon I'll hear his car door slam. I know soon I'll hear his boots on the porch. I know he'll be back, looking like his father, looking like his father these days. I know I'll sit my son down and feed him soup.

Bad Girl on the Curb

THERE IS A BAD GIRL ON THE CURB. IT IS 2:30 IN THE MORN-
ing and I, like a good girl, have been sleeping since midnight.
My husband has been awake on the couch, reading a book
about earthquakes, sipping whiskey from a short glass, and it
is he who comes into the bedroom to wake me up and let me
know about the bad girl. But I know about her already, having
been awoken by her crazy brakes and screeching tires. "What
happened?" I say, pulling the sheet up over my nightgown,
covering the thick scar I haven't yet let him see.

"There's a bad girl on the curb," he says.

"What'd she do?"

"She hit a parked truck, and now she's sitting down sur-
rounded by cops. Come on. Check it out."

I think about taking the sheet with me onto the balcony,
but instead say "Give me a minute."

Michael shakes his head, insulted, and walks out of the bedroom. He tips the glass this way and that in the hall and I hear ice cubes knocking against one another. There were hurtful things I said to him just days after my diagnosis, perhaps as a test, and I think of them now, cranky, accusatory words falling from my lips, and the expression on his face, a forty-year-old man, stunned on a waiting room couch.

I hear the sliding glass door open and know that he's standing outside in the wind and cold in just his cotton pajamas. I think of bringing him a sweater, going to the closet and pulling out one of the knits my mother made him six months before she died, the blue one or the brown one, but decide against them both. There are gestures I talk myself out of these days, ones that I'm afraid will encourage him to come in too close. More than once he has sat at the breakfast table with a cup of coffee, a half-filled glass of orange juice, the newspaper spread out in front of him, and I have stood behind him, unnoticed, and stopped my own hand midair as it went for his shoulder. There are positions I avoid in sleep, spooning him would mean my one good breast against his back, and him spooning me might mean his palm searching for what's no longer there. I am careful where my feet go. I fold myself into something small and wake with my elbow or shoulder half off the mattress.

Now I put on my robe and join him. On the dark balcony, I reach for his hand. He pulls it away. "Sure, Sara, now that we're not in bed," he says sharply. "You don't trust me."

"It's not trust."

"You're beautiful to me when you gain weight, when you've got the flu—what have I ever done to make you think—"

"This isn't the flu."

"No, it's not."

"It killed my mother—"

"It won't kill you," he says.

"We can't predict—" I begin.

"*Exactly*," he says. "We can't predict, Sara." He runs a hand through his hair, shaking his head.

"Okay," I say. "I'm sorry," I tell him. "Let's look at the girl. Didn't you want me to come out and look at the girl?"

And the girl looks bad all right, sitting on the curb in her black dress, her long hair down, strands of it hanging in her face. The streetlights glow orange, and she sits with her back against the post directly across from us. We live on the third floor and even from up here, at this hour, there's a lot one can make out. Not quite the look on the girl's face, but the way her thin knees meet and the high-heel shoes she holds with one hand, and her bare feet.

"She's glowing," Michael says.

"I bet she's freezing."

"She needs a sweater."

"You need a sweater too," I say, touching his sleeve. "Let me get you one." I turn to go inside, but he takes my hand.

"Stay out here with me," he says, smiling. "The drama is warming me up."

We stand quietly a few minutes until I finally say, "I'll be myself again soon. I promise."

"Good," he says. "Because I miss you."

"It takes time."

He's nodding, moving closer, still holding my hand.

"You'll see," I say, turning around and looking into the living room. It's lit up in yellow light and I see my husband's blue slippers on the hardwood floor, the throw pillow at the far corner of the couch, and the earthquake book he was reading sitting in the pillow's dent where his head must have been. I see the bottle of whiskey and a silver bucket of ice, tongs half in and half out of the bucket. I see the map of California's faults he's got spread out on the coffee table. "Are we any closer to being able to predict them?" I ask.

"It's a new science," he says. "The author calls it a baby science, a newborn discipline. It's a lot about what we *don't* know, which is cool."

"Sounds frustrating."

"Not really," he says. "Also, there are these people who think they know when an earthquake is going to strike. They say they can feel vibrations in their bodies or something. One woman gets a pain in her foot and is convinced that China's about to crack."

"Whenever I see that Lucy-woman seismologist on the news, she's trying to convince some reporter that she doesn't know anything, that nothing is certain."

"Sort of like having cancer," he says.

"Let's not talk about it," I say, feeling my muscles tighten, my back and shoulders stiffen.

"You could outlive me, is what I'm saying."

I shake my head, look back out at the street where one of the cops is placing flares and another one keeps a watchful eye on the bad girl. Every few minutes the girl tries to stand or move or escape and the cop comes and steers her back down. I don't know what he says to the girl, if he calls her *Dear* or *Missy* or uses her first name. I don't know the tone of his voice or how hard he grabs her arm. The truck is smashed, bumper thrown off onto the grass, taillight torn and hanging like an earring.

There are things about me my husband does not know: how many nights I was drunk too, running into cars and men I didn't know were there. How I've imagined my own tumors every day for years, fat cherries or plums, how I believe my own worry and predictions inspired the first foul cell. How I was always so sure about my fate. "She must be really drunk," I say, stating the obvious.

"She was wobbling before you got here."

"Poor thing."

"Maybe if *you* had a drink or two, Sara, you'd let me see. You'd let me in."

I turn away from him, look once more at the girl. "I bet her heart is broken," I say. "I bet someone broke her heart tonight."

"Maybe," he says.

"I bet no one asked her to dance."

"Could be."

"All her friends had dates. All her friends were dancing with handsome young men. She sat on the bar stool alone— for a long time, song after song. And she felt ugly, unloved. She kept drinking. What do you think she was drinking, Michael?"

"I don't know."

I nudge him.

"What?"

"Play along," I say. "Play with me," I tell him.

"Okay." Michael pauses. "Let's see, she was drinking those fruity martinis maybe—those green or yellow horribly sweet things."

"Apple or lemon," I say, smiling.

"Lemon drops, yeah. She drank one after the other."

"And another one after that!"

"Yes," he says.

We're quiet a moment, staring into the street, not looking at each other. Maybe Michael's wondering about what's going on beneath the earth in front of our building, the plates shifting and threatening our tall building by the sea. Maybe he's wondering if I'll withstand the chemotherapy or if I'll crumble like that bridge in San Francisco. I remember watching the news, seeing the pictures—the bridge sliced in several pieces, a little blue pickup truck heading toward the edge.

"I bet she doesn't care what happens next," I finally say.

"In the morning she will."

"When she's sober."

Then the girl is up, arms out like wings, trying to touch her nose. Within moments she is walking a line, tipping left and right. I imagine she wants her bed or mother, a glass of water or one more sweet drink. The cops are big in their dark clothes, towers pointing flashlights at the girl's unsteady feet. Halfway down the block from the scene, neighbors have gathered in little groups under trees, a young man and woman leaning against a fence. An old man with a big poodle stands by a fire hydrant.

Michael leans over the ledge to get a better look, and my first impulse is to stop him, to pull him back up where he's safe, but he looks bold and brave bent like that, a human question mark. He stares down at the bad girl and makes sympathetic sounds, his tongue hitting the roof of his mouth. "Poor thing. She's in trouble," he says.

They point the girl toward the police car. The back door is open, a waiting cave. She shakes her head frantically, says no so loud that we can hear. "She's feisty," Michael says, just as the two officers are helping her inside—one with his hand protecting her head as she dips into the backseat.

The girl's palm is pressed flat against the window as the car pulls away from the curb. She looks anything but feisty now, I'm thinking.

"Her hand," Michael says. "Did you see her hand?"

"Yes," I say, leaning over the ledge too, joining him. The groups of people are breaking up. They've seen enough. The poodle lifts his leg to pee. The young couple steps away from the fence. They're holding hands, walking into the apartment building across the street. My husband looks up at me and at my chest. I look too. My robe has slipped open and revealed to him what they left me. It is ours. Whatever happens next happens to us.

Grip

THE MAN AND WOMAN WERE IN THE KITCHEN, MAKING coffee. He wore thick socks and blue boxer shorts. She wore a white robe. It was 8:00 a.m. and the sun came in through the blinds, lighting the kitchen and making stripes on the table, chairs, and tile, making stripes even on the man's face as he stood at the sink, his hands curled around the counter. He was looking out the window at the empty driveway. The car was parked along the curb. It annoyed him that she left it there again.

Put in an extra tablespoon of beans, he said.

The woman held the grinder in her hand, her thumb on the button. Aren't you worried about all that caffeine? she said. What if it makes us nervous, what if we can't go through with it?

We'll be okay, the man said, whether or not we drink strong coffee.

The woman put the grinder down, then scooped another tablespoon of beans from the foil bag. She was thinking about a man friend from work, a man she'd recently kissed by the copy machine. She put the beans into the grinder, then pressed the button with her thumb. She listened to the sound of the beans breaking apart and wondered what her man friend's body was like under his blue suit. She knew his chest was hard because she touched it through the fabric.

Not *too* fine, the man said, turning and looking at the woman.

What?

Don't grind the beans too long.

What's too long? she asked. I grind them until they're ground up.

Last time you made them into powder, he said.

Right, the woman said, taking her thumb off the button. Great, she said.

It fucks up the coffee, he said.

I only made them into powder because you were yelling at me, if you weren't yelling the coffee would have been—

I'm not yelling now, the man interrupted. Would you like me to?

The girl was three years old, asleep in her pink room. There were toys on the floor—blocks, a stuffed bear, and an ABC book. Though the girl was very smart and knew the alphabet, she was a sad girl and frowned easily and often, for long periods of time. It didn't seem to her that the man and woman loved her; it had always been like that.

The man and woman sat together at the table, drinking their coffee.

I knew it, she said, frowning, shaking her head.

What? he said, irritated now, already, this early and irritated for the second time with the woman. You don't like coffee, you like hot water. That's what you'd rather be drinking here—hot, dirty water, he said.

The woman put her cup down and pushed it toward the center of the table. It's too strong to enjoy, she said.

I don't understand why we can't have one morning when you don't complain about the coffee. The man felt the muscles in his neck tighten. He felt his shoulders stiffen. He wished he'd married someone else, someone quieter, or he wished he hadn't married anyone at all.

Because I don't get to make it my way. It's like everything, she said.

After the man finished three cups of coffee, the woman rinsed their cups. She stood at the sink, the light on her then, lemon soap on her hands and wrists. She hummed a song he didn't recognize.

What's that, he said, what are you humming?

The woman stopped humming. She didn't look at the man.

Where'd you get that song?

In my head. I don't know where it came from.

He didn't believe her. Are you having an affair? he asked calmly.

What kind of a question is that—having an affair? Shit, she said.

Within the hour, the two of them dressed, then went to the girl's room. The man had half of his body—his chest and one of his arms—inside the girl's closet, looking for her second tennis shoe.

Fuck, he said, where's her shoe? Where'd you put her shoe? Why can't you park in the driveway? What's a driveway there for? Why do you park the car along the curb? His face was red and sweaty. There was a visible purple vein on his forehead.

The woman said nothing.

She can't go without her shoe, the man continued.

Calm down, you need to calm down, the woman said. She stopped buttoning the girl's little jeans. She exhaled, then walked to the closet. Here, she said, the shoe is here, under her clothes. The girl sat quietly on the bed. The woman came back and finished buttoning the girl's jeans. The man stuffed the girl's feet into the shoes. He tied them. Tight.

The girl's feet ached in the tight shoes. She looked at the man's face, searched for something she couldn't name. My feet, she said.

What? he said.

The girl said nothing.

•   •   •

They drove down Spring Boulevard, the man and woman in the front seat, the girl in back with her white bear. Anyone watching the three of them would have guessed they were going on a picnic or to the beach, to an amusement park or relative's home. It was a perfect day for such an event; a soft, dry heat warmed the car windows.

I need to get these brakes looked at, the man said.

Yeah, the woman said, they sound bad. It's dangerous. I read about a guy just yesterday whose brakes went out and he ran his car right into a building downtown. Killed three secretaries.

What happened to him? the man asked.

Broken toe, she said. Maybe take the car in this week.

Where does the time go? the man said.

I'll take the car in for you on Monday, she offered.

You'll get ripped off. They'll take one look at you—that sweater, that skirt—

Stop it, the woman said. You'll upset her, there's no need to upset her now.

The girl was holding her bear. One of its eyes hung by a thread. Two weeks earlier, the woman tried to fix the eye. She planned to cut the thread, then sew the eye back on. She stood with the girl's bear under her arm, scissors in one hand. The girl screamed and screamed, mucus above her lip, on her chin.

Don't kill my bear, the girl begged.

Fine, the woman said, let the eye hang there. You're going to lose it, she told the girl.

In the car, the eye fell off, into the girl's lap. The girl picked the eye up and put it in her pocket. The area where the eye had been was whiter than the rest of the bear. The girl thought this was curious, the way the eye protected that spot, kept the spot cleaner and softer. The girl touched the whiter area with her fingertip.

They got on the 405 Freeway going south and the man and the woman looked at each other. She shook her head.

Think about what you're going to tell your mother, the woman said. She's the one I worry about—always asking for pictures, wanting to know if she has your father's eyes.

I'll handle it, the man said.

Good, the woman said. I don't want to deal with *her* on top of everything else.

I understand that. He paused a moment. Let's not talk, can we just not talk? Let's just sit here, he said.

After driving many hours on the 405, passing beach cities and many shopping malls, the man pulled over, parked the car on the shoulder, and left the engine running. Wake her up, he said. And the man and the woman got out of the car. Other cars sped by, lifting the woman's shirt, exposing her belly. The little girl snored lightly. She gripped her bear. Wake her up, he said again.

The woman opened the back door. She shook the girl.

The girl was startled. She sucked in a bit of spit that was

falling from the side of her mouth. She wiped her face with the back of her hand. Are we here? the girl said.

Come on, come to Mama. The woman stepped back from the car, leaving room for the girl. She held the door by the half open window. Now, she said, we're here.

The girl had a bad feeling. She knew it would be better not to move, not to move from the car. She clutched her bear and turned to the woman. Where are we? the girl asked.

We're here, the woman said, this is where we're supposed to be. *Here,* she said, firmly.

The girl's lower lip began to shake. She put one tennis shoe in the gravel.

Now, the woman said, raising her voice.

The girl stepped out of the car.

The man walked around and got back inside. He did not look at the girl, he did not look at the woman standing with the girl, he looked at the windshield, into the sky at a billboard. The sign read: FINE RUM IS PURE PLEASURE. A man with dark hair sat in the sky with a blond woman on a couch. They each held a glass of rum. The woman's legs were long and tan and lovely. She wore a red dress. Her lips were bright and fat. The man in the car wanted to fuck the woman on the billboard, wanted to *be* the man on the billboard, holding a glass of rum, laughing with such a woman. He was thinking about the billboard, about sitting in the sky, when his wife jumped into the front seat, quickly locking the back door, then the front door.

Go, fuck, *go,* she said.

·   ·   ·

When the fire trucks arrived, the girl was gripping the wire fence. Her fingers, curled around the metal, were white—whiter than anything the men had ever seen. The girl did not move or acknowledge the men. Even the blond man in his twenties calling her Sweetheart did not attract her attention. She was concentrating on the fence, on everything the fence was, everything it offered her. She was concentrating on her fingers wrapped around the fence; she had never been like that, she had never been so strong.

The men put out cones, lit flares. Three of them gathered around the girl.

Please, Sweetheart, the blond man said. Let go. He picked up the one-eyed bear, wiped off the gravel, and held it to the girl's cheek. Please, he said again.

The girl gripped the wire fence.

My name is Adam, he said, I'm here to help you.

The girl stared straight ahead.

Adam placed his hand over the girl's hand, gently picking at her index finger, trying to peel the girl from the fence. Come on, he said, let go.

She clutched even tighter.

Adam rubbed the girl's arm. Sweetheart, he cooed, I'm sorry.

After several minutes, one of the men handed Adam a pair of wire cutters. He dropped the bear to the gravel, then held the cutters in his hand a moment, thinking. Cars and trucks slowed down, people turned their heads. Adam stood directly behind the girl, bent down, and began cutting a circle around her hands. He was thinking about the hands, about the white fingers, while he cut the circle. He was imagining how she got there, to that place, to that freeway, with her fingers curled around the wire fence, thinking how she held on with such strength, a little girl bigger than anyone, gripping tighter than any sweating man with a barbell, how she would not let go, not for him, not for anyone. He thought of his own baby at home in a blanket, sleeping with his little hands in a fist, why the hands grabbed, gripped the air—even when the boy was awake, in Adam's arms, how the boy held on, how he had to hold on, how his curled fingers were just the beginning.

What Milton Heard

THE WAY I LOOK AT IT IS YOU CAN'T BLAME A GUY FOR WHAT he might have heard. I'm not saying that I heard anything, but even if I did, I'm not taking the blame. You can't hold me accountable for what happened upstairs. My neighbor Duke is a big guy, chest and arms and back, and if you think for one minute that Milton Penny's going to be the one to tell him right from wrong, to tell him to stop doing *anything*, you're mistaken.

Have you ever taken a look at Duke?

Have you ever seen his eyes?

What happened upstairs in Duke's apartment was his personal business and really if I *had* heard anything—which I'm not saying I did—what was I supposed to do? Bang on the ceiling with a broom handle and tell the guy to stop?

And how upset do *you* get when a little girl or prostitute is killed? I'm pretty sure you've got other things on your mind, personal matters, and that I'm not the only one who doesn't go to candlelight vigils or doesn't hold office in the Community Watch Club. Who's got time to cry about every kid or woman murdered that he does not know? Not me, that's for sure.

Maybe you're in a recliner now, in an apartment twice as big as mine. Maybe you're looking up from your lap, moving your eyes from May's issue of *Sports Illustrated* to your pretty wife, who's pointing and sighing at the television, and maybe you follow her lead and look to the set. Maybe the newscaster is saying, *He's killed six girls in the last year. Oh terrible,* you think to yourself, sucking a bit of air in and out of your mouth for expression. You look lovingly at your daughter—the girl playing with her blocks in the center of the room—and then at the dead second grader's picture on TV, telling yourself that she was in a bad spot at a bad time on a bad lawn on a bad street, and that your little angel could never end up on a milk carton or in an out-of-the-way motel room with that man. Certainly not now because that man is in trouble, sitting in his cell, maybe on his knees, saying a tardy prayer. *Good,* you think to yourself, *he can't hurt anyone else.*

And that's how it was for me, like you watching the news, only the news happened above my head, in Duke's apartment, and I wasn't even sure what was happening up there. And, unlike you, I don't have a wife or a daughter or a living room full of blocks.

I'm on the couch, opening a bag of corn chips with my teeth. I'm sticking my hand inside the bag, scooping chips into my palm, when I hear them banging at the front door. Moments ago I heard them on the stairs, their boots and growls, their big voices. There must have been ten of them, a SWAT team, and now there are two cops on my doorstep, asking questions. They stand in their blue uniforms, asking me if I know Duke, what sort of neighborly relationship do we have. Does one of us borrow sugar or flour from the other? Do we drink beers together? Do we watch football games or share secrets? Do we talk about sex? Swap stories? Do we tell each other what we like?

"What we *like?* Want to clarify that?" I say.

"Who you like," the short one says. "You know, tall women, short women, girls, youngsters? Maybe you like men?"

"I like women, thank you very much," I say. "Don't go accusing me of being homosexual," I tell them.

They want to know if I saw any of the girls going up the stairs. They call me by my first name. "Milton," the short cop says, "you must have seen something. What about ears? You got ears?"

"I got ears," I say.

"You hear anything?"

"Huh?"

"A scream, Mr. Penny? Did you hear anyone screaming, struggling upstairs?"

I tell the cops that I didn't hear a thing, that Duke is just a guy who lives above me, that I don't put my nose where it doesn't belong. The cops nod. The tall one with the great, long face smacks his lips. They look at each other and then back at me.

"Duke is just a guy who lives above me," I say again. "A good neighbor. A quiet guy who keeps to himself. Just a guy who lives above me, that's all."

"*Lived,*" the tall cop says. "He *lived* there, but not anymore, you understand? He's elsewhere, you get me?"

Shorty says they'll be back. "Don't leave the area," he says. "Stay put. You hear me?"

"I hear you."

"You're not planning a vacation, are you? You're not off to the Bahamas or anything?" he says, and then he backs his elbow into his tall buddy's ribs, gently, playing. The two cops laugh. They stand in my doorway laughing.

"I take vacations," I insist. "What's so funny?" I want to know.

On Monday I hear from a group of neighbor women that Duke killed six girls in the last year and a half and that he did the killing right in his apartment. Imagine that, twelve feet up, right above my head, girls were being killed. The last little girl was related to the mayor. They had an eyewitness. Someone saw Duke holding the girl's hand, leading her and her chocolate bar into a yellow Toyota.

The big woman with lipstick on her front teeth asks me if I'd heard any strange noises coming from Duke's apartment, and if I had, why hadn't I done anything to stop the bastard? "You could've saved a child's life," she says. She looks at me like I'm the one who did the killing. I watch her red, waxy teeth as she speaks, wondering the whole time why the lipstick stays there like that, why her skinny lip doesn't suck it right off.

"No," I say.

"No, what?" she says back.

"I didn't hear a thing."

"I'm sure you did," another hen says.

"It was quiet up there," I insist. I'm looking down, talking to the sidewalk.

"It's terrible," the woman with lipstick on her teeth says, "what happened in your building. I hope you know that. You've got your own god to answer to, don't you? You have a god, right?"

"Yeah."

"Good," she says.

The women cluck their tongues, shake their heads. "I'll pray for your soul tonight, that's what I'll do," the big one says. Then all together, like dancers, like Vegas showgirls, the women look at me and lift their painted eyebrows toward the sky.

"That's good," I say, meaning it. "A man can't get too many prayers said on his behalf."

"You're a liar, Milton Penny," a skinny woman squawks. She's crouched down on the cement, a real nut, I'm thinking. She's peering out from behind the bigger woman's thigh. She gathers her housedress at the neck. I see one of her fluffy slippers, a bony ankle, and the net on her head meant to hide her pink curlers.

"I see your curlers," I say. "Right there." I'm pointing at her head.

"You're crazy," she says. "Look how fast you talk. We all know how crazy you are." She pulls the net tighter around her head, but still I can see.

I point again where a curler is coming loose. "You're going to lose one," I warn, and sure enough, as she's reaching up to save it, the pink tube drops from her forehead and rolls in my direction. When it taps against my shoe, I figure it's mine. I bend down and pick it up. "Finders keepers," I tell her, satisfied.

"Something's terribly wrong with you," she says.

I put the sticky curler in my pocket and look at her.

"Give it to me, you lunatic!" She's growling now, a real sight.

"It's mine," I say, walking away.

At the end of the month a young couple moves into Duke's apartment. On moving day they introduce themselves as Matt and Shelly. He props a box up on his hip and sticks out his hand for me to shake. Shelly sets a lamp down on the bottom stair and pushes hair out of her face. I'm at my front door, saying hello, welcome. I shake Matt's hand. I smile at the girl. They smile back, then return to their moving.

At my front window, I hold the curtains to one side and watch the couple lift boxes and pillows and bundles of books from the back of a red pickup truck. Matt's muscular with glasses and long hair. He says things and she laughs. She steps into the truck at one point and hands him a huge plant that covers his face, so he's nothing but jeans and sweatshirt and leaves.

I can tell that the girl is a college student because she has that look about her, that college look. It says she's better than I am, that she knows things I can't even imagine. When they enter the building again I let my curtains fall and return to the door. I stare out the peephole waiting, watching her calves flex their way up the stairs.

Shelly's breasts are big and high, and smart or not, they make her look cheap. Even days later, with her notebooks against them, they are there, those big breasts, spilling out from behind a manila envelope and loose papers, confessing something. She wears small skirts with bright-colored sandals or little black boots. It depends on the weather, what is on her feet. Matt wears suits and carries a briefcase. He pulls that long hair back into a neat ponytail. I assume he's a liar, that his hair isn't the only thing he's dishonest about.

For the first few weeks they're nice enough, almost friendly, saying hello in the hall, at the door, before going up the stairs. But after living in the building just one month I guess they're tired of all that. They stop with the pleasantries. Shelly's icy when I see her on the street. In the garage Matt looks less than happy to see my face.

One day in the laundry room Shelly's folding her silk panties into a triangle when I walk in with a duffle bag full of dirty clothes swung over my shoulder. I make a point of letting the door close on its own, and when that doesn't get her attention I clear my throat. I deliberately cough. Shelly doesn't look up, just goes about her business. "Hey," I say.

Shelly says nothing.

"Hello there."

Still nothing.

"How's it going?" I try.

She keeps folding panties, one pair and then another. She makes a silk pile and doesn't look at me.

I put my duffle bag on top of an empty washing machine and shake my head. "Did you hear me?" I say. "I said hello," I tell her.

"I heard you," she says, her voice flat.

"Well?"

Shelly shrugs. She's wearing white shorts and a blue halter top. Her shoulders are tan and freckled; they rise and fall when she shrugs for a second time. "*What?*" she says, exasperated.

"You having a bad day?"

She rolls her eyes.

"It's okay," I say. "You're feeling unfriendly, not in the mood for chitchat, no big deal," I tell her.

"Look," she says, "you're creepy."

"Maybe so," I say.

"You stare, you peek out from behind curtains. Let me do my laundry in peace." She places her panties in the laundry basket on top of a stack of neatly folded towels. "And *stop* looking at my underwear," she says, picking them up again and stuffing them to the side.

I look away from her, stare at the radiator in the corner.

"Something's wrong with you," she says.

"You've been talking to the hens?" I ask her.

"Who? What hens? What are you talking about?"

I open the washing machine and begin dumping in my

things. "You're being very rude," I say without looking at her. "There's a minimal amount of courtesy a man like me expects."

"A man like you?" Shelly shudders.

"That's right."

"Well, *a man like you* creeps me out. You're always staring. I can't stand it. Jesus," the girl says, gathering her sheets and pillowcases into a messy bundle and dropping it on top of the towels. She carries the basket with both hands, then kicks the door open with one of those sandals. "Christ," she says on her way out. "Give a girl some fucking breathing room."

David Letterman is in the hospital having heart surgery. Sick ticker. I know a thing or two. I keep up. My own television might be broken, but I read the newspaper. So the voice I hear coming from the couple's apartment isn't Letterman's. It's probably some hungry comic that is secretly hoping for Letterman's death. It's a voice I don't recognize, but the words are clear, as is the laughter and applause.

It's after midnight and I want company. I'm in the mood for friends I don't have. I've taken a beach chair out of the closet, unfolded it in the far corner of my living room so that it's now directly under the couple's set. I sit in the chair and listen. As I concentrate I feel vibrations from the laughter above throughout my whole body; it is almost like being touched, a million tiny fingers.

The imposter makes a joke about a fat woman in a string

bikini on Malibu Beach, how fat the woman was, how everyone on the sand was offended by the woman's fat. Matt laughs and laughs. I laugh with him, quietly, into my hands. Shelly is silent. I see her in my head, sitting on the couch in just a T-shirt, braless, those big tits humbled, hanging. I see her sulking. I imagine myself their good pal, on the couch too, between them, our six knees all in a row.

I see Shelly leaning over and hear her apology in my ear. Her warm breath on my cheek. Hand on my shoulder. "I'm sorry about the laundry room," she says. And she's got excuses: *my cat died on Sunday* or *it's that time of the month.* She offers me crackers and soft cheddar, a peppermint from a little dish.

"I'm sorry, Milton," she says again.

I thought the little blond girls were one girl, Duke's niece—that's what Duke told me and the little girl didn't object. She smiled shyly and held his hand. He nudged her and the kid curtsied on the steps. Seemed like a niece to me. Seemed like a well-behaved kid. How was I supposed to know that Duke was taking the girl upstairs to kill her?

In the morning the cops come by again. It's 7:00 a.m. when they knock on my door. The short one insists that I must have heard Duke murder the girls, says something about the manner in which they were killed. "We know more than we did last month, Mr. Penny," he says.

118

"Well, good for you."

"There's evidence of a struggle, some music being played."

"And?"

"Do you know anything about Bach or Mozart? Did you hear music like that coming from Duke's apartment?"

I shake my head.

"You okay?" the long-faced cop says.

"Why the long face?" I ask him.

"Jesus Christ," he says. "Do they pay me enough for this?"

I'm looking at Shorty's navy uniform, watching the dark buttons pull away from the fabric, staring at the exposed bit of white T-shirt, thinking that this guy should eat less, that donut shops and greasy diners are killing him.

"Stop staring," he says.

"Jesus," the other one says again.

I smile at them.

"What did you hear, Penny?"

"Nothing," I hear myself say, moving my eyes from the man's belly to the buttered toast I'd been eating before they arrived.

"What did you hear? Just tell us what you heard and we'll be on our way."

I pick up the piece of toast and take a bite. It crunches in my mouth and I wonder if they can hear it.

"What's that?" Shorty says, pointing at the hen's curler. It's standing up on the mantle, balanced there, a pink tower, still sticky if someone were to touch it.

"You got a lady friend?"

119

"Sure," I say, chewing and talking at once.

"That's great," he says, unconvincingly. "Wonderful. Now, tell us about Duke."

"What did you hear?" they ask again, their faces moving toward mine. An inch or two more and they could kiss me—they're that close.

Waste

SKIPPER AND I ARE HAVING PROBLEMS. HE'S DISSATISFIED.
It's all there in Skipper's face, in his flushed, unshaven face, all
the problems we are having, all his dissatisfaction. Sometimes
I ask him questions he doesn't answer. Sometimes he balks at
my comments or ignores them altogether. He scrunches his
eyes together and doesn't even look like Skipper. Oh, Kara, he
might say, as if I were a child and he doesn't have time to
explain the world to me.

We've been together for six years with good sex two to
three times a week and decent conversations, then last Sunday
morning over coffee and blueberry muffins, his face changes
shape; he's hard to recognize. Really. And he looks at me and
blurts out that he's never been happy with me, that I've never
made him completely happy. He says that I've never fully satisfied him, sexually, that is. Emotion might be here. Comfort.

There's an ease between us, yes, but sexually, he's not getting what he wants.

I tell him that he's the best sex I've ever had and besides that, there's love here. Right, I tell him, right? Emotion, that's love, isn't it? You're talking about love when you say "emotion."

And Skipper looks over my head, out the window, maybe at the palm fronds outside the window, and says nothing.

Later, that same Sunday, Skipper returns from grocery shopping in the early afternoon, and I'm standing in the kitchen pouring wine into glasses, wearing his favorite black teddy. I help him unpack the groceries and feel silly putting away milk and onions and cheese in such an outfit. Skipper sets the toilet paper on the table. I hand him the razors and soap. It's fine, he says, you look great. But his face looks odd, like he doesn't mean it.

We sit on the couch, drinking. Skipper doesn't look any more familiar and I don't feel any less silly. This was a bad idea, I say, and remind him of what he said earlier.

What can I do? What do you want me to do? I say, and as soon as the words leave my lips I regret them.

You could pee on me, Skipper says, if you loved me, you would pee on me.

Skipper thinks all our problems stem from the fact that I refuse (have always refused) to pee on him. If you did this one thing for me one time, Skipper says, you'd see that it's okay, you'd see me love it, and that would make it okay for you, better than okay. Skipper says that he's never loved anyone as much as he loves me and that he's never asked anyone else for urine. And that's why, Skipper says, he's never been peed on. It doesn't occur to Skipper that the other women he slept with but didn't quite love might not have peed on him either; I am the only woman in the world selfish enough to refuse him.

Debra would have peed on me, Skipper says, nostalgically.

Then why don't you ask Debra? Why don't you call Debra right now, this minute, and ask her? I say.

Because I didn't love Debra the way I love you, he explains. I didn't trust her the same way.

Maybe you should have, I tell him.

Pee isn't such a big fucking thing to ask for, Skipper says. And he puts his wine down and walks to the den.

A couple days later I'm eating lunch at Sam's Seafood with my best friend Anna. Anna has just finished telling me about her new lover, Linda. Linda, Anna says, is the most gifted woman in the world. Linda, Anna says, is the most generous. No one gives like Linda, she says, winking. Good, good, I say absently, and I must look upset—maybe my face too is changing shape under all this pressure—because now Anna won't let up. What's wrong with the two of you? she keeps saying. And I surprise myself when I blurt out, Skipper wants me to pee on him, he's always wanted me to pee on him. I tell Anna that Skipper's blowing this pee thing out of proportion, that he's blaming my refusal for his every unhappiness. Anna is trying not to laugh. She raises the napkin to her mouth and pretends to wipe something away. And the laugh is there, there in her napkin.

Is this funny? I say. Anna, what the hell's so funny? Skipper's face is all skewed up into a stranger's face, he wants my urine, and you're laughing.

I'm sorry. I'm really sorry, Anna says.

I tell Anna that I can't pee on Skipper, that I can't imagine my life without him, but I can't imagine peeing on him either. If I peed on him, I say, I wouldn't be able to look at myself, talk to my mother on the phone, or pee the same way again.

Anna puts the napkin in her lap. She leans in. Maybe there's something else wrong with the two of you, maybe Skipper's using this pee thing as an excuse to leave you, maybe it's symptomatic, she says.

He really wants the pee. He's wanted it from the beginning. You just don't know, I tell her.

The waiter pops out of nowhere and sets two bowls of creamy soup in front of us. He smiles oddly at me, like he knows, like he stood somewhere listening.

Can I get you anything else? he says. Perhaps some water?

I think I see a smirk. We're fine, I tell him.

Once the waiter's gone I panic.

Did he hear us? Do you think he heard us? I ask Anna.

Who?

The waiter, did he hear what we were saying?

Don't worry about it. It doesn't matter.

But if he heard—

Anna interrupts me then and says, You can't worry about what people think. You just can't worry. She picks up her spoon. I read about a man once who would only have sex with his wife if she barked like a dog. Imagine, barking like a dog—for your husband, she says.

This is different, I say.

Maybe, she says.

The first year Skipper and I were together, I thought he would grow out of this urine thing. I thought it was more a fantasy than something he really wanted. The night he brought it up, we were in bed, my head on his stomach. I was looking at the wall, noticing the cracked, yellowish paint. If this room's going to be *our* room, I said, we should paint it. What do you think of one red wall?

Red walls drive people insane, he said. It's been proven.

What about a rose color then—a pale, pale red?

Maybe, he said. And moments later, with his hand in my hair, he asked, What do you think about urine?

Urine?

Urine.

We'd had a big fight and just recently recovered from it, so I'd returned to that stage in our relationship where I wanted so badly to be loved by him, and said things, not necessarily reflecting my own feelings, but things meant to please, to entice, and to mystify him.

I've never thought much about it. What about it?

Do you think it's ugly?

Not really ugly. Necessary, I said, urine is necessary.

Do you think it's sexual?

I'm not sure. It might be sexual.

And later, watching him sleep, watching his square jaw, his barely open lips, I remember thinking, *this man wants my urine*. And I was oddly flattered—that he would want even my waste. I thought him not a freak, but an enigma. An enigma, however, I would refuse and refuse and refuse. An enigma I am still refusing.

Had he insisted that night, I might have crouched and let go, might have balanced my eager hips above his stomach or crotch and given him that. But he did not.

After lunch, Anna and I stand outside the restaurant.

Is this about control? Anna says. Is this about staying pretty?

You don't understand, I say. It's something Skipper wants that I don't want just as badly.

It'll be okay, Anna says, holding my shoulder.

He's growing a beard, I say.

I thought you hated beards, she says.

I suppose it could be worse. Skipper could ask me to kill some-one. Or he could ask me to tie him up and stick pins in his feet. Or he could ask me to bark before sex. Demeaning, that's what barking like a dog is. And I suppose peeing on him isn't half as awful as him wanting to pee on me. You don't want to pee on me, do you? I asked him a year ago. No, he said, I just want to be peed on. Still, I'm not about to pee on anyone, not even Skipper.

Skipper says that I won't pee on him because I'm worried about society, what the world thinks, what the world would think if I peed on him. He says people are miserable, that they shoot each other on freeways, torture each other in dark rooms, judge each other for all bad reasons, and all he's asking for is a little pee. He says people think and worry too much about what others are doing in bed, and the reason, he says, is because they're so dissatisfied with their own sex lives and worse, he says, they hate their bodies and their bodies' functions.

Peeing, Skipper says, is a glorious function, and you're too fucked up worrying about the world to enjoy it.

It's just not sexual to me, I say. It's waste, I remind him.

You've been poisoned, he says.

When I was in college I dated a bartender named Anthony. Anthony was tall and handsome, with brown curly hair, and older—nearly thirty. His hands were smooth and tan—the fingers long and elegant. I sat at his bar one night and watched him pour drinks; I was excited by those fingers.

I was twenty and all my friends had boyfriends. I wanted a boyfriend. I wanted more than anything for Anthony to be my boyfriend.

On a Friday night I went to Anthony's apartment to watch movies. He'd promised me a musical and what I got was a lengthy porno film. Near the end of the film, a naked woman lay on wet grass, in the middle of a meadow maybe, and a man in an orange cape carrying dynamite approached her. The woman had yellow hair that fell across her cheeks. Hair like straw. And the man stood above the woman, looking down at her, at her naked body, at her straw hair. He said one word. *Open,* he said. He stuck the dynamite inside the woman and began to whistle. He lit the dynamite. The dynamite sizzled and crackled and the man continued whistling.

I sat on the couch next to Anthony in my short black dress, watching him watch the woman, watching him watch the dynamite, listening with him to the sizzling and crackling. When the woman blew up, the caption read: The Big Bang. And Anthony laughed and laughed, a big, deep laugh from the bottom of his guts. I hated him then. I felt the hate on my face. It was hot and red; I thought he could see it. I tried hard to wipe the hate off my face, still hoping Anthony would like me. Would touch me. Would be my boyfriend.

He started grabbing at me, at my neck and hair, at my skirt. And I was dry inside, all dry, no matter what Anthony did with those lovely fingers. And I remember thinking: We are ugly and deserve each other; we deserve *this.* Then I helped him with my zipper.

When I tell Skipper about Anthony, Skipper shakes his head. This urine thing is not about violence, he says. I don't think sticking dynamite inside a woman is sexy, Kara. Don't confuse me with that bartender.

There are lines I don't want to cross, I say.

I am not that bartender.

I know, Skipper. The man in the movie whistled.

I don't want to hurt you, he says.

I think it was a show tune, I tell him.

On Saturday night Skipper and I have dinner at Anna's. With Anna and Linda. We eat bread, salad, and pasta. White sauce. Anna is glowing, there is bright light all around her. I look at Linda and wonder if she knows Skipper wants me to pee on him.

I watch Anna watch Linda.

I watch Linda watch Anna.

Skipper leans toward me. Part of love *is* objectification, he whispers emphatically.

I drink glass after glass of wine. Every glass is a preparation. I'm ready for a fourth. I follow Anna to the kitchen. I ask her to open another bottle. She's wonderful, I say, you've never looked happier. Do you like Skipper's beard?

I think it looks good, she says. But you hate it, don't you?

I'm going to pee on him tonight, I tell her.

Are you sure? Is that okay for you? If not—

Tonight, I interrupt her, is pee night.

Is that enough?

Pee night, I repeat.

Why are you drinking so much?

Preparation, the peeing person must prepare, I say, and I laugh, all the way back to the table I laugh.

On the way home, in the car, I am not laughing. I am looking out the window at the road, at the black trees. Skipper has one hand on the wheel and one hand on my thigh.

What if I wouldn't fuck you, what if I loved you, lived with you, did everything sexually for you, but wouldn't fuck you? Would you stay with me, would you be satisfied? he asks.

Yes, I say.

But would you miss it, the fucking part? Would you want me to fuck you?

It depends.

Would you try to talk me into fucking you?

Yes, I tell him.

We are in bed. The pillows are fat against the headboard. The sheets are white. Crisp. Skipper is naked. I wear a blue silk gown. I am kissing his neck and ear. He is touching my hair, moaning softly.

What do you think about urine? I ask him.

I lay him down on his back. I drink the glass of water I've brought into the bedroom. I drink it down, simply, easily. I set the empty water glass on the nightstand. Skipper is breathing hard now, astonished. I am crawling on top of him, enjoying this. I start to lift off my gown.

No, he says, leave it on.

I pull the gown up, gather it at my waist. I crouch above his stomach, near his crotch, and let go.

As the hot urine falls from my body onto his body, down

the sides of his body, on the white sheets, I am overcome with anger. I try to stop peeing, I try for the sake of us to stop, to stop this peeing, but I cannot.

And moments later, Skipper is on me, moving inside of me. The gown is wet and tight and tangled about my waist. I am looking at the empty water glass. Skipper is looking at my cheek, kissing my face—grateful. I feel his beard, his red and brown beard, his new beard. The room is pungent. My gown is pungent. Thank you, Skipper says, thank you. And as I move with him, loving him, I am leaving him. I will leave him. It's as sure as anything.

Eggs

LILLY'S MARRIED MAN WHO LIVES SIX STATES AWAY ALWAYS calls on Monday mornings from his office on campus—7:00 her time, 9:00 his. She stays up late on Sunday evenings watching reruns of *I Love Lucy, Cheers,* and *M*A*S*H,* so that she's sleeping when his call comes. So that his ringing is the first thing she hears, the first thing in the morning, the first day of the week. She imagines what he looks like when he talks, what he's wearing, what he's doing with his limbs. Often his voice is low and cajoling. It's the kind of man he is, she believes, feeling the need to soothe her even before they begin.

"I'm fine," she tells him. "We're not even lovers," Lilly says. She imagines him in Levi's, black heavy boots, a white button-down shirt—the one she saw him in last, the one she started to unbutton on the hotel balcony ten months ago, then changed her mind. She sees the boots up on the desk, his ankles crossed.

He stares out the window and tells her about his office and the earth there: a fig tree, the red brick buildings going brown against the rain, a sophomore boy who has a crush on him, who stands outside in his football jersey without a hat or an umbrella, madly biting the inside of his cheek. There's an old, slow computer that sometimes freezes up. Papers everywhere, thrown about the room, like confetti at a party. Books, an antique globe, and a small aquarium with a half dozen fish.

"We're friends," Lilly says. "It's what friendship is—men and women talking, liking each other—without the sex. It's what we have here."

"Not quite."

"We haven't even kissed."

"We talk about it enough."

"We don't talk about kissing," she says coyly.

"I'm frustrated," he says.

Lilly turns on her side, her breasts falling against each other. "Me too. I'm sorry," she says.

"It's not your fault," he tells her. "I'm the bad one. I'm the married one." And then he lowers his voice even more. "I don't know. Maybe we should stop all of this."

"Stop what? Stop talking? God, no," she blurts out, and then realizing what she's said, quickly adds, "If you'd feel better, okay. I mean, I'd understand. I really would," she says, unconvincingly.

It's a conversation they have a couple times a week, on Monday mornings and on Wednesday mornings too, before Lilly leaves for work, and it's followed by confession, admission, phone sex, and always guilt—him coming toward her and pulling back, her letting him. Him in his office with his palm in his Levi's, and Lilly in her sheets, her own fingers on her thighs. It's something she thought she'd never do, masturbate with someone on the phone, and each time, after she comes, she's shocked at what has happened.

"What's the boy look like?" she asks him now.

"Tall, dark hair."

She knows she should cut this conversation short, that she's got papers to grade before school. "What's he wearing today?" she asks, unable to stop herself.

"I don't know," he says. She hears his body twist in the chair, the shades being raised. "He's not here yet," he tells her.

"Let me know if he comes."

In addition to the jock who loves him, Lilly has heard about his wife as well. She wears his ring and feeds his babies. She crawls next to him at night and rests her dark curls on his chest—the chest Lilly's not yet seen. She knows his hands, their veins and small scars, in ways Lilly does not, though she saw the left one inching toward her face on that hotel balcony. "Don't," she'd said.

He held his hand in the air a second before letting it fall to his side. He looked at her, defeated.

"I'd be in less trouble if you touched my hip or leg."

"That's strange. I'm not sure that makes sense."

"It's terribly intimate, don't you think? It's meaningful somehow." She paused, uncertain. "I wouldn't be able to forget it, that's all," she said softly.

"I understand." He rubbed his palms on his jeans. "It's an impulse. I'm attracted to you. I feel something," he told her.

They met at a summer conference for English professors in Arizona. They stood up from their hard chairs at the exact same moment, nearly tripping into each other, leaving a particularly boring rhetoric professor aghast.

"Did you see the guy's mouth," he said, "just hanging there, open? He could have caught one of these bugs in that open mouth of his." He motioned to the winged thing that had made its way into the hotel lobby.

"Jesus," she said, "what the hell *is* that?" And just then, the buzzing thing went flying into Lilly's hair. "Help. God, get it off me," she said, jumping about.

"Hold still." He reached down, pulled whatever it was out by its wings, and let it go.

It was 10:00 a.m. and they began with Bloody Marys. By noon they'd switched to beer, and by 2:00 they were standing on his balcony. He said he'd slipped, sleeping with one other woman in his ten years of marriage. He said he'd felt incredible horror and shame, that it wasn't worth the sex, how terrible he felt. He'd met her in a depression support group.

"You're depressed?" Lilly asked him.

"Isn't everyone?"

"I don't know." She rested her elbows on the railing. "I've never thought about it like that. Sometimes I'm depressed."

"That's what I mean," he said, "sometimes."

She leaned over the railing.

"It's a long way down," he said, reaching for her.

She laughed at his nervousness.

"I'm sort of afraid of heights," he admitted.

"That's charming," she said.

"Fear's not charming," he said.

"Admitting it *is*." She looked at him and smiled. "Did you see a lot of her?"

"Who?"

"The woman you slept with."

"No," he said. "Just once."

"You never called her back?"

He shook his head.

"Now. *that* must have depressed her."

"Good," he said, "you're quick." And then he inched his hand toward her face and she backed away.

They stared at the brown and red Arizona hills, more of those winged bugs they couldn't name, and a massive cactus for several minutes before talking themselves out of it, off of the balcony, and heading downstairs. They decided to continue whatever it was they started or finished through e-mail or the phone.

"Safe," Lilly said.

"Perfectly," he agreed.

"The boy's here," he says now.

"What's he wearing?" Lilly sits up, fluffing the pillows, then stacks them against the headboard and leans back.

"Let's see," he says, and then she hears the chair squeak, and the shades again. "He's got that jersey on. It's blue, and he's getting wet. It's pouring. It's really coming down hard."

"Why doesn't he use an umbrella? I don't get it," she says.

"Neither do I. Why does he stand out there at all? I'm married. I'm straight. I've never given him any reason."

"Maybe you should say something to somebody."

"Okay, *now*," he continues, "he's sitting down—right in the mud. Jesus. He's under that big tree, just sitting. He's going to be filthy when he gets up. He can't go to class like that. How can he walk around campus?"

"Can he see you?" She glances at the clock by her bed and realizes that she barely has time to take a shower.

"He's not looking my way."

"Maybe he's not interested in you anymore. Maybe your charm has worn off," she teases.

"Oh shit," he says, "he's looking now."

"Tell me about him again."

"He was in my Twentieth-Century Lit class a year ago and has been following me around campus ever since. The pub, the cafeteria. I'll turn around in the quad and there he'll be. Last week he was even behind me in line at the market."

"Maybe you should tell someone," she tries one more time.

"He's not dangerous. He doesn't really say anything, and if he does, it's just, 'Hey, what's up?' or 'How's it going?' The kind of questions kids ask when they really don't want an answer."

"He might want an answer from *you*. That might be exactly what he wants." She clears her throat. "Sounds scary to me," she says.

"I'm telling you, Lilly, usually the guy just stands there. I'm sure he's harmless. It's a crush. It happens. I'm sure you know all about student crushes."

"I know a bit about them, yes. But this guy sounds like a stalker—showing up at the supermarket, staring into your office window."

"I'm sure he's harmless," he says again. "I've told you all this," he says. "Don't make me repeat myself."

There's a student this semester that's troubling Lilly as well, a matriculating graduate she doesn't mention to her married man. The woman is a bully, and Lilly feels small and inadequate in her presence. Penelope is much older than Lilly and bigger too, thick hipped and heavy breasted, well read and overly confident in her opinions. She wears a fat gold stud in her nose that she twists, Lilly's noticed, when she's particularly irritated.

Sometimes when Lilly makes a point in class, she catches Penelope shaking her head, disagreeing. "You're wrong there," Penelope might say, madly twisting the stud. "Did we read the same book of poems?" she might ask, snidely. And once, "You misinterpret things, Dr. Lyle. You misinterpret poems and then you try to pass that misinterpretation on to us. You want us to go out into the world when we're done here and repeat the stupid shit you say?"

Lilly tries to remind herself that Penelope is the student and that she is the professor. She makes the rules and gives the grades.

It's easier to ask her married man about the harmless boy who follows him and pretend that Penelope doesn't exist.

But she does exist, and is, in fact, the first student in the classroom every Monday and Wednesday morning. There she sits, first row, middle, tossing her long gray hair over a sturdy shoulder. Always, she drops her backpack on the desk to her left and hangs her leather jacket over the back of the chair to her right, discouraging other students from sitting down next to her. What Lilly hates most is what she sees then for the whole hour and a half of class: Penelope, arms crossed, long, thick legs shot out in front of her. Penelope framed by those two empty desks. It freaks Lilly out, the smile, the shoulders, the nose ring, the way Penelope looks at her with disdain and takes up more than her allotted space in the world.

One night, after more than Lilly's limit of red wine, she asked her married man too many questions, so she knows more about his wife than she should. She's Lilly's age and height, around her weight. Her hair, like Lilly's, is dark and long and curly. Her eyes, like Lilly's, are green. They're the same astrological sign. They come from divorced homes. Their mothers are dead. They wear a size 8 dress, both of them partial to the color dark blue. Once a week they sit on their beds with pumice and lotion, softening their feet. They paint their nails and lips red. Opium is their perfume of choice.

"It sounds like we're twins," Lilly said.

"Not at all," he said, and then he went on to complain. "She's obsessive as hell. She'll like something, say, a movie or book, and she'll read it or see it a thousand times, again and again, until she's quoting the damn thing, until it's all she knows to talk about. She loved that ridiculous film about the idiot. The one that came out years ago. Tom Hanks and that box of chocolates," he said. "What was that called?"

"*Forrest Gump.*"

"Yeah, Gump, the idiot. Jesus, what a sentimental piece of crap. Did you see it? Oh, she's moody as hell, too."

"Yes, I saw it."

"And her feet are ugly, no matter what she does to them," he continued.

"I'm moody," Lilly said, "and you've never seen my feet."

"Well, all that astrological stuff is bullshit anyway."

"What about the rest of it?"

"You look nothing alike," he said. "I'll send a picture."

"Don't you dare. I don't want a picture. Why would you think I'd want a picture?"

That's when he told Lilly about the eggs. He said that his wife stands at the stove in an old robe, thread hanging from the falling hem, and cooks them. Egg after egg. Sometimes she'll scramble up a dozen and call it dinner. Sometimes she drops them in boiling water like her mother did. Sometimes she fries them with a bit of cheddar on top. Morning, noon, and night. It's what they're eating now, all of them, for nearly every meal. Sometimes there's toast and potatoes, and sometimes there's just more eggs.

"It's what she does," he said, "when she feels unloved." Then, "This has got to stop. I can't eat these damn eggs all the time."

"No," Lilly told him, "you can't."

"Shit, they're awful. You put ketchup on them, salt, red pepper even, you fold them up in a piece of buttered toast, it's still a fucking egg," he said.

"Why don't you say something?"

"I do. She cries," he said, "and then she won't stop. I'd rather eat the eggs than watch her weep and scream—deal with that whole mess. Jesus, I'm sorry—make me stop talking about her. It's a terrible thing to do—to you, to her."

"You're talking because I'm asking," she said, lifting the glass of wine to her lips, drinking the last bit. "Why don't you make something else—for yourself and the kids at least?"

"It would kill her," he said, "if I didn't sit down and eat them."

"Too many eggs will kill *you*," Lilly told him.

She knows about the four babies as well—his two sets of twins. He showed Lilly pictures in Arizona. He flipped his wrist, the baby photos protected by plastic, spilling out of his wallet. He stood there on the balcony, twelve inches of pictures hanging from his palm. Babies in pink, babies in blue—the four of them dressed identically in little yellow suits. Babies at the shore. Babies on a kiddy slide at the park. A baby with chocolate on his or her chin. "Here and here and here," he said, beaming. A dad.

"Pretty," she pointed to the second photo.

"Those are the boys."

"Well, they're pretty regardless."

She was lying of course—those big-jawed boys, like the big-jawed girls surrounding them, looking like something pre-historic, dangerous. Lilly was wondering how he bounced babies like that on his knee at all. And her nastiness surprised her—what she felt and didn't feel for his children.

Years ago Lilly felt something, or told herself she did, for babies she hadn't seen, for a family she didn't know. Her friend Desiree was having an affair with a married man. She needed Lilly's ear. They were sitting out at Desiree's pool, drinking iced tea, and she was confessing. Lilly was the first friend she had told. "I can't tell the others," she said. "They're married. It's like a fucking club. No matter what they say, they'd hate me. I tried telling Kate. I explained all of it. And you know what happened?" she said.

"What?" Lilly said.

"The next time I went over there, she hid Bernard in the other room—that fat, impotent freak of a husband."

Lilly smiled.

"She thought that *any* married man would do, even hers. Jesus. It made me sick." She paused. She took a deep breath. "He's got kids," she said, finally. "Two of them—and maybe one on the way."

"*Maybe?*"

"They're not sure if she's pregnant again, but she's late."

Lilly was shaking her head, saying, "Des, I can't believe

142

you're doing this to *a family.* He's lying to you. That's what married men do. A woman can spend her whole life loving one and end up alone." She didn't understand Des's situation and was giving her only what she'd read in magazines, the weak generalizations she'd gleaned from daytime television. "Think about holidays. You want to spend every Thanksgiving alone?"

Desiree poured more tea in Lilly's glass. "You wait—if it happens to you, you'll understand."

"I'd *never,*" Lilly assured her.

"So self-righteous," she said, looking at her hard. "I'd expect more from you—all those books you read."

One day in workshop, Lilly is commenting on a student poem, asking, as she always asks, where the heat is, what the student is doing right, and Penelope shakes her head and snickers—it's not a laugh and not a giggle, but a fucking snicker, Lilly thinks to herself. And she doesn't want to sound defensive in front of the others, but hears her voice, as it rises, becoming weighty and stiff, like armor.

Lilly, from six years' experience, knows that when a student dislikes you in the special way that Penelope dislikes her, it can infect a whole class. She senses this particular group dismissing her ideas easily now, and though she's charmed and even wooed disrespectful students in the past, here, she finds herself speechless and sputtering.

More than once her imagination has taken over. She's

feared the students were armed, imagined them packing guns and blades, a .45 deep inside a backpack, a hunting knife slipped into a sock. Those days, she doesn't take off her jacket for the entire hour and a half. She stares at the door and reminds herself that it is there.

Last night's *I Love Lucy* was the one where Lucy's recently given birth to Little Ricky. The one where Little Ricky won't stop crying, and Lucy and Big Ricky, Fred and Ethel, gather around Little Ricky's crib and start cooing. Fred cooed the most; his cooing was the strangest. The show was a comedy, but Lilly wasn't laughing. She was frightened. His cooing was odd, and a close-up of his bald skull inching toward the baby's crib made Lilly turn down the volume and look away. She stared into her bedroom mirror and didn't quite recognize herself: thirty-five, alone, with mascara smeared under her eyes. They looked like him, those four babies, especially the girls, the masculine jaws on their small faces. On the nights she misses him most what occurs to her is that they're nothing more than burping flesh, a nuisance, and worse, she sees him in her mind, packing up his shirts and jeans and books, heading west, never once looking back at those ugly babies.

When they talked themselves off of the balcony they focused on three things: the ring on his finger, his rejected mother, and Lilly's too. They acknowledged the women in their lives who were left by men like him, standing on balconies in faraway cities, reaching toward the faces of women like Lilly.

"We can have a friendship," he said. "Send e-mail, talk on the phone. I mean, men and women *can* be friends."

"Of course." She leaned away from him, and they watched the trees and rocks and mountains—everything dry and brown.

"It's hot," he said.

"There's no breeze now." She waved her hand in front of her face. "Not even a little one. How does anyone live in a place like this?"

One Thursday Penelope comes by Lilly's office and knocks on the half-open door. "You busy?" she asks, entering without waiting for an answer.

"No," Lilly says, looking up from the pile of papers she's grading. "I can talk to you now."

"Damn straight," Penelope says.

"It's my job, I mean." Lilly is flustered. She wants the woman to go away.

"That's not very flattering."

"Leave the door open, please."

"You afraid of me?" Penelope asks.

"No," Lilly says quickly.

"Seems like you're afraid of me—that's why I asked."

"I'm not afraid of you," Lilly says, trying to stay calm, reaching up to make sure the buttons on her blouse are secure.

"I don't think you're very smart," Penelope says matter-of-factly, as if she's commenting on the weather. "A lot of teachers I've had here at this school aren't very smart, but you, you may very well be—"

"We're not teachers," Lilly says, having had enough. "We're professors."

"Same thing."

Lilly shakes her head. She sighs. She leans back in her chair, getting as far away from Penelope as is possible in the little room. "What do you want?" she asks her.

Penelope drops her notebook on Lilly's desk. It's red leather or a cheap imitation, Lilly's not quite sure. If it were another student's property, Lilly might look at the notebook more closely or even touch it, but neither of these things she's willing to do.

"My poems," Penelope says, gesturing with her chin. "Read them."

"What?" Lilly's taken aback.

"Read them," she repeats.

"Maybe you should find someone else to read these," Lilly says. "A professor you respect." She pushes the notebook away so that it's half on and half off the desk, a precarious piece of shit, Lilly thinks. A cheap imitation of leather that's cold to the touch, she tells herself.

"It's your job, Dr. Lyle. I did the work and it's your job to read them."

"You need to behave," Lilly says.

"Behave?" Penelope scoffs.

"Yes, you need to act like the grown-up you are."

"I'm a grandmother," Penelope says, taking in a deep, audible breath. "A grandmother with a pierced nose and navel, but still a grandmother."

Lilly says nothing. She drums her fingernails on the desk,

thinking about other problem students she's had in the past: the stammering boy who told her to f-f-f-fuck off when he didn't like his C; the pretty junior who tried to kiss her in the parking lot; the kid who was always, every day, an hour late. Lilly decides that Penelope is somehow the worst of the bunch, the most unsettling.

"I'm a grandmother," Penelope says again.

"I don't care what you are," Lilly tells her.

"Don't they pay you to care?" Penelope says.

"No," Lilly says, wearily, "they don't."

"What's his name?" she asks her married man, curling up in her bed, touching her right nipple until it grows hard.

"Who?"

"The boy. The kid in the jersey."

"Oh," he sighs. "His name . . . I think it's Jonah."

"You think?"

"Yes, I think so."

"It's a pretty name."

"I guess."

"Do you think the boy's pretty?" she says.

"I've never thought about it."

"Never?"

"Not once."

It occurs to her then that her married man is a liar, that he wants to fuck Jonah like he wants to fuck her, and she wonders what else he's not telling the complete truth about.

"What's the boy's hair like?"

"I don't know. Long," he says.

"Like yours?"

"I guess."

"I thought you said he's a football player."

"He plays ball, yeah."

"Don't football players have to wear their hair short? Don't they have rules?"

"I don't know about the boy. Enough about the Goddamn boy. Shit," he says.

Lilly sits across from the head of the English department, listening as Dr. Jay Davis tells her about the complaint. "I know Penelope Walker isn't the most pleasant student, but she's very smart," he says.

"She might be smart, but she's a terrible poet."

"Really?"

"Intelligence doesn't always equal talent."

"Well, either way, Lilly, you need to read her work, the work she's done for the class. You can't refuse to read her poems."

"She's incredibly rude, Jay."

"I've heard that before," he said. "But you're the professor here. You're the one in charge."

Lilly nodded, wanting suddenly to cry.

"Penelope says that you're refusing to read her midterm. That she wrote her poems and you won't look at them." He gestures with his eyes at Penelope's notebook on his desk, as if he, too, doesn't want to touch it.

"She's a bully," Lilly says. "It seems like there should be a code of conduct or something."

"Yes, well—" he begins, but she cuts him off.

"Doesn't seem right that she can march into my office and insult me and I still have to read her crap," Lilly says.

Dr. Davis smiles.

"She thinks everyone here is an idiot. Even you," she continues, surprising herself.

Dr. Davis stiffens. He adjusts his tie. He doesn't want to hear such things, she can tell. "It doesn't matter what she thinks," he says. "It's too late in the semester for her to transfer out."

"Give me those," Lilly says, picking up the notebook. "Fine," she says.

Years ago, when Lilly was a girl, her mother worked the night shift at the hospital, and Lilly was often left alone. One night she was on the couch watching *James at 15*—a '70s drama about adolescent angst. It was a particularly moving moment—James about to dance his first dance with a girl he adored. She wore a short dress, Lilly will never forget the print—yellow wildflowers against a blue background. James leaned down and offered the girl his hand and the girl reached up and accepted. And Lilly thought about a boy she liked at school, Edwin Jackson, and how he'd looked at her earlier that day. She imagined that her life would be full of moments like the one portrayed on television, romantic moments made up of offers and questions and coy nodding and answers and dancing, so much dancing.

The next day at school Lilly and her friends crowded in a bathroom stall, passing a joint around, discussing James's first dance. "Did you see her dress?" Lilly said. "Those fancy flowers?" Becky stood directly on the toilet, white tennis shoes on the white seat, and she was tall then, towering above the others like royalty.

"I need gum," Desiree said. "Anyone have a piece?"

Becky leaned down and smiled, holding the pink wad between her upper and lower teeth. "Want some of this?" she said, pulling it in half.

"Gross—*ABC*," Lilly said, "*already been chewed.*"

Becky rolled her eyes. "You're scared of everything," she said. "Germs, boys, basketball. I'm surprised you smoke pot."

Desiree looked at Becky, then at Lilly, then back at Becky. She took the tiny bit of gum from Becky's fingers. She held it for the briefest second, deciding, then raised it to her lips. "Edwin Jackson likes you, Lilly," she said, chewing. "Or at least he wants to fuck you," she said.

After she hangs up the phone with her married man she calls Desiree. "I'm sorry," she tells her, "about you and John. I should have been more sympathetic," she says.

"John who?"

"*Married* John."

"That was three years ago, Lilly. You're calling me about it *now*?" She yawns into the phone. "It's early. What time is it? It's my day off."

"I'm sorry I judged you."

"Be sorry you called me so early," she says.

"Remember when you took the gum from Becky, the piece she'd already chewed?"

"What are you talking about?"

"In seventh grade. We were in a bathroom stall, the four of us, smoking pot, and you needed gum—maybe so that Mrs. Grayson wouldn't know you'd been smoking—and Becky offered you hers."

"I'd never have taken gum from that slut's mouth," she says.

"You did, Des. You put it in your own mouth and chewed. And then we finished the joint."

"I don't know what the hell you're talking about."

"The gum," Lilly insists, "it was pink."

"That's crazy."

"There's a student that hates me."

"There's always some little brat," Desiree says.

"She's not little. She's an old woman and she's hateful," Lilly says.

"Go to sleep, Lilly," she says. "Or let me get some sleep at least. Let's talk about this tomorrow, okay?"

Lilly says nothing.

"Lil, you there? You there, Lil?"

"I'm here," Lilly says, but she isn't at all sure.

•   •   •

151

On Wednesday afternoon she meets her graduate students for workshop. Mary, the best writer in the class, is up. She passes out copies of her new poem and then begins reading aloud. It's about molestation—as many of Lilly's students' poems are these days. They write about rape. They write about sodomy. They write about uncles and fathers and older brothers. They write about dark rooms and little beds with men in them who do not fit—hairy ankles and feet hanging over mattresses, soft white bellies and sour breath.

Some of the other students are tired of these poems. "It's like watching the same stupid movie over and over again," Jarred told Lilly. "Soon it's just one more kid with a bullet in his heart, one more chase scene, one more crash. It's like that," he said.

In Mary's poem, the father enters the daughters' bedroom and moves from one twin bed to the next, from daughter to daughter, until his favorite one stirs and does what he demands: a hand job. And for this she is grateful, her mouth empty for the first time in three nights. As she reads, a couple students are obviously unimpressed, bored even, sighing, moving in their chairs.

"That's not how it happens," says Penelope. "*Please,*" she says, rolling her eyes.

"Let's talk about form," Lilly says. "Content later."

Mary shakes her head. Even from her desk, Lilly can see her eyes are wet, that she wants to speak.

"In a minute," Lilly tells her. "Hang on."

Penelope won't let up. "It doesn't matter what shape this

152

poem's in—if the speaker is full of shit, she's full of shit." She tosses that gray hair of hers and lets out a big breath—as if the air's been inside her lungs her whole life. That's how it sounds coming from her mouth, as if she's been saving it up for an exasperating moment such as this.

The poem is good, Lilly thinks, Mary's most original work.

"Let's try to talk about what the poem is doing right," she says, but her voice is uncharacteristically tiny, cracking into the room.

"Aren't you tired of reading these Daddy-fucked-me poems?" Jarred says, looking at her. "Aren't you tired of them?" And then he looks over at Penelope, and she lets out a laugh and he lets out a laugh back, and they're both laughing, roaring it seems to Lilly, moving back and forth in their chairs.

Mary moans then, a deep moan—a sound Lilly's never heard.

"She's tired of remembering," Lilly says. "She's tired of confessing, confiding, tired of looking into your vapid faces," she tells them, and her voice is big, echoing into the classroom; she could be ten women. "And I'm tired of *you*," she continues, moving out from behind her desk, walking over to Penelope. She looks into her eyes, those thin lips, and stands over her, shouting, "What the hell do you know about anything, *bitch?*"

"I've been given a temporary leave," she tells her married man the following Monday.

"What happened?"

"I'm going to finish my book."

"Right in the middle of the semester?"

"Let's not talk about it," she says.

"It just seems like—"

"*Please, please,*" she begs.

He pauses, says nothing for several seconds, then finally, "Why don't you take a trip? Why don't you come here for a weekend—or longer. We can meet up in that pink motel I told you about and just talk. Whatever you want," he tells her. "Whatever you can handle."

"I can handle all of it."

"What are you wearing?" he asks suddenly. "Where are your hands?"

"Nothing," she says. "I'm naked," she tells him, opening her robe.

"Touch yourself for me," he says.

Lilly arrives at dusk. The cab driver taking her from the airport to the motel introduces herself as Brenda. She wears black lace, and Lilly can't help thinking that it's not quite safe for her to dress like this and drive a cab. Still, it's pretty. Delicate and dark. "That's a beautiful blouse," Lilly says.

"Thanks. I bought it at a garage sale. Just twenty bucks." Brenda smacks her gum and raises her eyes to the rearview mirror so that Lilly can see.

"Is it safe? I mean, wearing it while you work. I saw your bra a minute ago—when I was getting in," Lilly tells her.

"Safe?"

"You know, driving men around."

"They give me mostly the girls—the girls on business trips. Like you," she says. Then, "I'm going to a party when my shift ends."

"It's none of my business. I'm sorry," Lilly says.

"What brings you here, to the middle of the country?"

"I pushed one of my students," Lilly blurts out.

"My God," she says. "What did he do?"

"It was a *she*."

"Wow. Goddamn," and then she lets out a little sigh and moves about on the vinyl seat, making noise. "Should I be afraid of you?"

"No," Lilly says. "The woman has a stud in her nose. She pierced her nose. What kind of woman wears a stud in her nose, at that age?"

"You pushed a girl because she wore a nose ring? My kid wears a nose ring. Jesus," she says.

"I pushed her hard, too."

Several minutes go by. The sun is slipping away, and there's nothing but brown earth and freeway outside Lilly's window. Trees zipping by—the same tree again and again. Miles and miles of the same damn tree. "What's it like, living here?" she asks.

"Let's not talk," Brenda says. "A girl like you with anger like that—let's just drive and not talk. I'll get you where you're going, but that's it," she says.

"I'm not a *girl*," Lilly says. "I'm meeting my husband."

Brenda is nodding. There is a long black thread hanging from her sleeve, and Lilly has an urge to pull it, to watch the blouse unravel into nothing, but she resists. She sits back and tries to stay quiet. It's difficult, though; she wants to talk. She wants to talk like she's not wanted to talk in years. There's so much Lilly could tell her.

"I'm sorry," Lilly says again.

The woman says nothing.

"I didn't mean to scare you," she persists.

Brenda's breathing so hard that Lilly can hear that string moving up and down her pale arm.

The motel is pink like he promised. There's a pool with huge dead bugs floating on top of the filthy water: a butterfly, two moths, and several beetles. The vacancy sign is lit up, flashing, and Lilly stares up at it a minute before sitting down on a plastic lounge chair. She lets her hand uncurl from the bag's handle and leans forward. A pair of dark blue panties sit at the edge of the pool near the steps, near the shallow end. She sits for several minutes, looking over at the panties, the crotch, thinking that you can live your whole life believing you're one kind of person—the kind of person who wouldn't do a certain thing, who wouldn't meet him here, who wouldn't push a student out of her chair, who wouldn't take ABC gum from another girl's mouth—and then suddenly you are, you are just that person, taking the gum from her fingers, lifting the hard bit to your own lips, putting it in, and it's not so bad, less sweet perhaps, used, and it's nearly erotic, and you feel almost sexy, chewing it, making it yours.

Soon he will come. Soon he will give Lilly something: flowers, candy. Something. Across town, his wife is making eggs, egg after egg. Her feet are bare, callused, yellow like yolk. His ugly babies sit with their forks poised, waiting for the evening's eggs, wondering what they will be tonight—sunny-side up or scrambled or poached.

The Study of Lightning Injury

ONE YEAR AGO MY HUSBAND MACK WENT CAMPING OUT on the Kern River with his best friend Cooper and the two men were struck by lightning. The Monday morning storm was unexpected, a surprise. At about 10:00 a.m., the way Mack tells it, the thunder woke him. He got out of his sleeping bag and stood outside the tent. The bolts were white. The sky was purple and blue and black as if someone had taken huge fists to it.

Mack was still angry with Cooper from two nights earlier, from Saturday night's confession, angrier than he'd even been on Sunday, the day after, but reluctantly decided to search for his old friend. They'd been buddies for twenty years. "You don't just throw twenty years away," my husband told me.

Earlier that morning, Mack had feigned exhaustion, rolling over in his sleeping bag when Cooper shook his shoulder, then shook it again. Mack grunted and grumbled for his friend to go away. He placed the pillow over his head. "I didn't want to fish, Lydia," my husband explained, "I only wanted to sleep."

After looking at the sky, Mack returned to the tent. He put on his Levi's, two pair of thick socks, boots and jacket, and went to the river. Mack was walking down an embankment and Cooper was walking toward him. Cooper, who'd been so successful that morning that he wore a colorful scarf of fish around his neck. Cooper, who smirked, who carried a graphite fishing rod while the rain pelted his body. Cooper, who stepped toward his best friend, with his rod held out from his chest and into the air, taunting fate and chance, saying, "I'm a brave man. These things are dangerous."

The hair on Cooper's face was two days old, thick and black. His skin was ruddy, my husband remembers, and the smirk grew into Cooper's final smile.

Mack doesn't remember if he responded to Cooper's bravado or not, if he let out a laugh or a warning to put the damn thing down. "Careful, that thing's graphite," he might have said—or, "Look at all those fish, you lucky bastard." He doesn't remember if, in that final moment, he forgave his friend for wanting me or not—perhaps he hated him with more resolve than ever.

I imagine the air between them smelled like pine and wet dirt and the many trout Cooper had draped around his neck. It was the smell of winning, of power and bad weather, of the dinner they'd surely share that night around the fire.

Mack remembers a black, finger-shaped cloud rolling in

over them. Mack remembers a flash—no bolts, no thunder, just light.

Yesterday, at breakfast, Mack wanted me to learn a new word. *Keraunomedicine,* the study of lightning injury. He wanted me to be able to pronounce it. He pointed at me with his piece of toast, waved it just inches from my face. His lips were greasy with butter. He was chewing and talking at once. "Go on, Lydia," he urged. "Use it in a sentence."

I did not use the word in a sentence. I did not say it out loud. Instead, I put down my cup of coffee and looked hard at my husband. "How much longer is this going to go on?" I wanted to know.

"The study of lightning injury is pretty new. People don't think about it, Lydia—don't you care about that?"

"I care about that, Mack."

"Use the word in a sentence then."

"No—not at eight in the morning, not before work—I've got classes to teach," I told him.

"Fine," he said.

"Maybe if you got back in the classroom yourself, you'd stop thinking about it all the time. You know, if you had to do a lecture on Chaucer, maybe it would take your mind—"

"A lecture?"

"Yes, maybe if you stood behind a podium and made a point about something other than—"

"Not yet," he said.

"What if you started making things again? My desk has about had it. The office could use some new shelves."

"Take one look at me, Lydia. Take a good look. Are you looking?"

"I'm looking."

"And what do you see?"

"You," I said, weakly.

"It's not me," he said. "And you damn well know it."

"I'm sorry," I said.

Keraunomedicine might be largely unexplored, but these days my husband, the English professor on paid leave, is exploring it himself the way he once explored literature and my body; he's diving into books like *Lights in the Sky* and *Ball Lightning: An Unresolved Problem* and *Lightning Injuries: What Happens When the Sky Quiets*. He searches newspapers and the Internet. He writes down facts he finds particularly interesting on index cards. He uses a red pen and leaves these cards all around the house, in odd places, on top of the dryer, in the medicine cabinet, in the freezer next to the icy sirloin. Places where I'll find them and be surprised. I asked him why he leaves them in weird places—why not leave them in a stack on his desk?

"Lightning is about shock, Lydia," he said. It was another early morning. Last month, a Sunday. We were still in bed.

"Okay," I said, yawning.

"And memory."

"How's lightning about memory?"

"It just is." He looked around our bedroom, taking seconds with each item: the ash desk he'd made himself, the sheets his mother bought us two months before she died, the dresser and closets and blinds, as if he'd never seen them before, as if we'd just moved in, and all of this would take getting used to. He looked at me the same way.

"See, Mack, this is one of those things you say that I just don't understand. It's not *about* memory. Your memory might be impaired because of the strike—but lightning isn't *about* memory." I paused a moment, reached for him, and then stopped myself. I softened my tone. "Can't we just say good morning? Can't we just say, doesn't coffee sound good?"

"You brought it up," he reminded me.

"You're right," I said.

"You wanted to talk about the cards."

"I know, I know, but what frustrates me is that you don't say what you mean anymore—or I don't get what you mean—either way we're in trouble."

Mack rubbed the sleep from his eyes and shook his head. "Look, lightning's about what I can't remember—and what I can't forget, no matter how much effort I put into it."

"I didn't kiss him back. You might want to write *that* down on one of your cards—" I turned away from him, taking more than my share of the blanket. I looked at the wall for several minutes before giving up, rising, and getting out of bed.

• • •

Today's card says: *Lightning kills people by causing cardiac arrest. It does not vaporize them or turn them into ashes.* I find the card in the refrigerator. He's got it propped up against the carton of milk. When I hold it in my hand I notice the paper is cold—the condensation has left the edges damp.

Mack used to spend Sundays building things. In the afternoons he'd return from the garage, sawdust in his hair, smelling like a man who had worked. He'd come up and surprise me at the sink, his arms reaching around my waist. He'd kiss my neck, and sometimes we'd do it right there on the kitchen table.

Two nights before the lightning strike, Cooper, who'd been sober for over a decade, put away three dark beers before confessing to my husband his feelings for me. He told Mack he'd been rethinking the AA thing, the Higher Power bullshit, the forced abstinence, all of it, and then he opened the cooler and pulled out a six-pack. Cooper drank the beer slowly, smacking his lips and sighing. "I should have done this sooner," he muttered to himself. The fire spit and hissed at the men, and every so often one of them would toss a stick or a ball of newspaper into the flame to keep it going.

I guess the beer loosened Cooper's tongue, or perhaps he'd intended to confess to Mack for some time now, turning the story over and over in his head. Maybe that was the motivation behind the trip itself, but all I know is what I've been told: Cooper wiped his mouth with the back of his hand. Cooper sighed. Cooper shifted the legs that were crossed underneath him in the dirt. Cooper smoothed his mustache into his beard, looked at my husband and said, "I've always liked Lydia, and I like her now, and two years ago I tried to kiss her in your backyard."

Mack sat there, digesting the information.

"Sometimes, I think it's what broke Grace and me up—my feelings for Lydia. It's why I don't come around as often," Cooper said.

Mack looked at his friend.

"We—I mean, *I*," Cooper corrected himself, "never acted on it—except for that one time in the backyard. It doesn't matter, though. Feelings like that have a way of working themselves into your daily life—they affect the way you put on your boots and look at your wife." Cooper picked up a beer bottle near his foot and looked at it. He dropped the bottle to the dirt and continued. "When Grace left me, she said I didn't look at her the right way anymore. I told her she was full of shit, but really, it was true—I didn't look at her the right way and I didn't love her the right way and I—"

Mack had heard enough. "Where?" he said.

"Where?"

Mack looked down at his hand and realized he'd been squeezing an unwrapped piece of beef jerky. He lifted the wrapper to his mouth and ripped it open, then took a generous bite. He chewed and chewed, tasting the salty meat.

Finally, he tossed the wrapper into the fire and said, "Yeah, where?"

Cooper shrugged as if he didn't remember where his attempt took place or perhaps he shrugged because he didn't understand what Mack was asking of him.

So my husband said it slowly, what he wanted to know. "*Where* exactly—where in my backyard were you?"

"Under that big tree."

"Which tree—we've got lots of fucking trees."

"The biggest one—the one with all those huge flowers."

"And?"

"And she pushed me away."

"What did she say?"

"She said she loved you and always would love you—that she cared about me as a friend."

"What else?"

"She said I better not touch her again. I better not talk about my feelings, ever—she didn't want to hear it."

"That's Lydia," Mack said. With that, he turned away from Cooper and went to sleep.

By morning, though, the men were drinking coffee together, trying to get on with their fishing trip. They were there to catch something, Mack reminded himself. Cooper was frying eggs in a cast-iron skillet over the open fire. Mack watched his friend, the man's broad back and shoulders, his thick dark hair. It wouldn't have surprised him at all if I'd been attracted to Cooper, not one bit, he decided. My husband was grateful for the sounds around him—the noisy hawks, the sizzling eggs, Cooper's low humming—it meant he didn't have to say much.

Cooper had sobered up and was obviously guilty, serving Mack the three *good* eggs—the ones with the perfectly round and full and yellow yolks. Cooper himself ate the eggs with the yolks that he'd accidentally split open—the yellow was spread out and cooked, a dull and unappetizing mess. "Here, buddy," Cooper had said, flipping the good ones onto Mack's paper plate, "you take these."

That morning's fishing was uneventful—neither man catching a thing. Mack says that except for a few unsuccessful attempts to talk to each other, they were silent. Mostly they talked to themselves when baiting a hook or casting a line into the river. To themselves and to the trout they hoped to catch, they said things like *perfect, fuck yeah, please,* and *come on, tasty baby.*

They baited those hooks with what Mack described to me as fluorescent putty, a bright green wad meant to make the fish bite. "There's glitter in it," he said.

"Whatever happened to worms?" I asked him.

"Worms?" he said. "You want to know about worms, Lydia? Don't ask me about worms."

"I didn't kiss him back," I told my husband again. "He said it himself—I pushed him away."

Since the strike, Mack hasn't touched me—at all. He doesn't want his skin to touch my skin.

166

I miss our legs and feet meeting somewhere in the middle of our queen bed. Now, in the early mornings, I reach for my husband and find the bed's valley, so much space between us, and Mack himself curled away from me.

He explains that this is temporary and to be expected—his fear of me, and that it will pass, along with the blurry vision, skin rashes, headaches, and terrible pains in his calves. I want to massage those calves back into health, use my palms and fingers to knead them back to this world. Months ago, I reached for them, his two legs poking out from the sheet while he slept, and he screamed and shuddered and begged me to go away. "Where should I go?" I asked him.

"To the kitchen, to the living room, I don't give a damn," he said.

What I miss most are good-bye kisses. In good-bye kisses there is a sweet pessimism that Mack described to me in our first days of dating. I know to him they mean: *What I want you to remember if I do not live through today is this, my lips here, here.*

One of last week's cards was from Psalms. He left it for me in the bathroom, standing up, sandwiched between my body lotion and hairspray. *He sent out his arrows, and scattered them; and He shot out lightnings and discomfited them.*

Mack has said that what pisses him off the most isn't that Cooper held my face in his hands and placed his lips on mine, but that I didn't tell him what had happened. "I'm your husband, Lydia. You don't keep secrets, not from your husband."

"It was your birthday," I reminded him.

"Doesn't matter," he said.

"I thought it did matter—it was your fortieth birthday and I didn't want to spoil it."

"Well, it wasn't my fortieth birthday the next day or the day after that."

"You're right."

"That's a best friend and a wife under that Goddamn tree, and someone— *you*, Lydia—should have told me."

The card I find on the coffee table reads: *A person struck by lightning is not electrified. This false belief has tragically delayed lifesaving efforts and resulted in several deaths.*

Last week Mack and I went out for Thai food, which he told me he didn't remember eating. Star of Siam was one of our favorite restaurants, and when we walked in the doors, Mack looked around as if he'd never been there before. "You remember the place, don't you?" I said. "It's the food you don't remember, right?"

"Yeah, sure—I remember the place. It just looks different is all."

Kusa, our favorite waiter, went to shake Mack's hand, but

the look on my face stopped him mid-shake. "Let me get you a table in the back," he said.

We'd been seated about five minutes and were drinking wine when I asked Mack if he remembered what Kusa's name meant.

"Heart," Mack said. "Let's toast." He smiled and lifted his glass.

"To hearts." I reached for my wine.

"To Kusa."

"Yes, to Kusa."

When the food came, Mack looked at each dish curiously, especially the pad thai. He poked around the noodles with his fork. He stabbed at a shrimp, lifted it to his nose before putting it in his mouth, which is something he'd never done before— picky behavior the old Mack would have condemned. Soon though, he relaxed and dug in. He particularly liked the Crying Tiger, a red slice of beef, which before the strike he would have sent back, complaining good-naturedly to Kusa that the cow was still alive. Instead, he ate the rare meat hungrily.

In between bites, my husband wanted to talk. "What do you do with a friend like that, a dead guy you've loved for twenty years who wanted to fuck your wife?" His tone wasn't angry, but matter-of-fact.

"He didn't want to fuck me," I said.

"What then?" Mack dabbed at his chin with the white napkin.

"He said he liked me, that's all."

"Are you nuts, Lydia—are you absolutely crazy?" Mack

looked at the napkin, the pink stains, then held it up for me. "Look at that—blood. I didn't like that before, did I?"

"No, Mack—it made you sick."

"I'm different now. It's like—I'm wired differently."

What Mack tells me about that Monday morning is this: he came to on the embankment, flat on his back in the mud. He was unable to move his arms or legs for several minutes. The first thing he saw was the sky, those beaten-up clouds. He heard the wind and rain. His heart ached. He opened his shirt and found burns on his chest, red skin that had already blistered.

When he finally did rise, there was Cooper just a few feet away, his body spread out by the river, a gray puff of smoke coming from his mouth, trout everywhere, the graphite fishing rod in pieces surrounding him. My husband smelled burning flesh and hair and fish—a horrible combination of death and potential dinner.

This morning Mack and I are sitting on a black leather couch in an office downtown, across from Bonnie, our new marriage counselor. She wears her blond hair up in a tight bun and little black glasses, but she's not fooling me. I know she is beautiful. I know she hears this every day. I know her husband has never been struck by lightning, that he's probably across town now, trying a case or making a brilliant financial deal. I know he loves her and touches her. I know he kisses her good-bye.

The first thing Mack tells Bonnie is this: "If you can hear thunder, you are close enough to be struck by lightning."

"Very good, Mark," she says.

"It's Mack," I correct her.

"Okay," she says, straightening her skirt, looking at me briefly, then turning back to my husband. "I think it's good that you talk about your experience, Mack."

"He's not *talking*," I say.

"What's he doing then?"

"He's studying it. He's memorizing it."

Her body stiffens. She looks at me sternly. "That may be a matter of perspective," she says.

I cross my legs. I try not to roll my eyes at this woman.

"To the ancient Greeks," Mack says, "thunderbolts were lethal punishment from the gods."

"Interesting," Bonnie says.

"The Romans saw strikes as a sign of condemnation and denied burial rites to those killed. Imagine that," Mack tells her, "the damn sky kills you and then the town torches your body."

I've had enough. There are things I have to say. "Look, Bonnie, Mack's got problems with intimacy—he won't touch me. And memory—he writes things down on cards."

Bonnie gives me the second stern look of the day and once again turns to my husband. "Like I said, Mack—I think it's good that you're talking about your experience. Talking is something—a beginning."

"He's not *talking* about it," I say. "Talking about it, I understand. I would talk to my husband all day long about what happened to him. He's studying it—and leaving these freaky cards all around the house."

Bonnie tightens her pink lips into a line. She writes something down on a little pad.

"What am I supposed to do with these cards?" I say, pulling a stack out from my purse, smacking them down on Bonnie's shiny coffee table.

"Maybe you should read them, Linda," she says.

"I'm *Lydia*. Jesus Christ, what's with you, Bonnie? Can't you even get our names right?"

"I'm sorry, Lydia—maybe you should read them," she says again.

"I *do* read them. What do you want to know?" and now I'm shuffling through the cards, reading them aloud. "'Lightning strikes the earth about one hundred times every second'—did you know that, Bonnie? How about, here's one, 'About seventy-five percent of lightning strike victims are men.' Here's another, 'Lightning can span more than five miles, contain one hundred million electrical volts and reach temperatures of fifty thousand degrees Fahrenheit.' Lightning is hot as fuck, Bonnie—"

Mack interrupts me then. "Lydia," he says, "calm down."

"No, Mack, *no*," I say. "Here's another, here's my favorite, 'The best shelter during a lightning storm is a building with plumbing and wiring'—you hear that, Bonnie, if you're ever in a storm, make sure that you're near a toilet—"

"Let's go, Lydia," my husband says. He takes my arm,

which is something, he takes his fingers and wraps them around my upper arm, and yes it's a gesture reserved for mothers and unruly children, but he's touching me and nothing terrible is happening to him, nothing is happening to him at all except that his wife is following his lead, up and off the couch, out of Bonnie's office, down her hall, out her front door and into the day. Once outside he lets go of my arm and I stop walking.

"Help me," I say weakly.

He reaches for my hand this time and stares a moment at our joined fingers—again, nothing happens, no sparks or smoldering skin or cardiac arrest. He leads me to the car and helps me inside.

"What if you're never the same, Mack? What if you never forgive me?"

"Shhh," he says. "Let me go pay Bonnie. Let me go back inside and pay the woman."

Lightning strikes the Empire State Building and Sears Tower thousands of times each year.

We do not live near the Empire State Building or Sears Tower. We live in a small house on a quiet cul-de-sac in Southern California. We've got two bedrooms and a den, an office and a backyard patio. Books and magazines, artwork and ceiling fans. Shelves and tables and desks Mack made himself.

Our front yard is full of rosebushes.

At night the street lights go on orange.

Sometimes I pretend the buzzing telephone wires are bee-hives.

This morning I accidentally brushed against my husband in the hall and he didn't flinch.

The thing about memory is this: it distorts, it makes tiny schools huge, it makes dead men brilliant, it makes mothers into villains and good girls into whores.

I no longer believe Cooper's version of the story. I no longer believe my own. I'm not sure who tried to kiss whom. It may have been me under that magnolia tree leaning forward into Cooper, and he might have been backing away, respecting his friendship with Mack, respecting his friend's wife. He might have been saying, *No, Lydia, what are you thinking? Stop, Lydia, this isn't right.* It might have been Cooper's shoulders against the tree's thick trunk, me leaning forward still, persist-ent hands reaching for his chest, and it might have been Cooper shaking free, stepping away from me, reaching up and picking a white flower. Maybe there were petals by his dark boots. Maybe he wore a denim shirt and black jeans. Mack might have been in the backyard too, just around the corner, under the awning he'd recently built. Maybe he was squeezing lighter fluid onto the charcoal. Maybe he was calling for us. Maybe we ignored him. *Look at this, Lydia,* Cooper might have said, holding the magnolia in his outstretched palm, *a flower big as a dinner plate.*

174

Ludlow

JIMMY SAYS HE LOVES ALMOST EVERYTHING ABOUT ME.
Two months before we got married I asked him what about
me bugged him. He didn't want to say, I could tell.

"Nothing really," he said. He shifted on the couch, picked
up the remote control from the coffee table, and turned on the
television. I took the remote from his hands and muted the
news. He looked at me. "Nothing bugs me all that much,
Sugar. Honest," he said.

But Darlene Tate is persistent. "*Please*, Jimmy. Please." I
shot up from the couch and went to the kitchen, where I
opened a drawer and pulled out a pad of paper and a pen.
"Make a list for me," I said, excited, handing him the pad, asking him to write things down so that I could work on them.
"I'm all about self-improvement. Darlene wants to better herself," I told him.

The first thing he wrote down: *It bugs me when you talk about yourself in third person.*

"Really?" I said.

Jimmy nodded. He thought for a moment and kept writing. *It bugs me when you take things from my hands, like you just did with the remote. You've done it with other things too—magazines, a can of Coke.*

"Interesting," I said.

And once he started he didn't want to stop. *It bugs me when we're in bed and I'm just about to fall asleep and you ask me a question. Like, What do you want for dinner tomorrow or Are you asleep yet? Once one of us says good night in bed, let that be it. It bugs me when I'm reading or watching TV and Annie calls on the phone and instead of going into the other room to talk to her, you stay put and talk really loud.*

I was looking over his shoulder as he wrote. After that last one, I snatched the pad away from him. "Enough," I said.

"See," he said, laughing. "You grab things out of my hands."

"My turn," I said. "Let me make a list for you."

"I don't want a list," he said, pulling me to him and kissing me on the mouth. "I love you so damn much, Darlene. I'll live with all these things and more—that's how much I love you."

Still, I question that love, and am afraid that the only reason Jimmy married me last month is because he thinks I'm going to be the mother of his child, and yes, I'm pregnant now, this very minute, but I bet I won't be by midnight.

Let me explain.

First off, there's that bitch of a psychic who swore I wouldn't make it into my second trimester, who told me in a high squeaky voice that I was going to lose the fetus—that's what she called him or her, my baby, my little boy or girl, a *fetus*. I could have knocked her out right there. Then there's my mother's history, and her mother's history, and her mother's mother too. We're women who lose three or four babies first before we're blessed—that's the way my grandmother puts it.

It's Tuesday, the last day of my first trimester, and we've been married exactly twenty-six days and three hours. We got married quickly, downtown at the courthouse on 6th Avenue, with only my friend Annie as a witness, because neither of us believe in abortion, or rather Jimmy doesn't believe in abortion and I didn't want another one.

Ten years ago, long before I'd met him, I'd had one, and then five years ago I'd had another, and then two years ago I had one more. These are three secrets from Darlene's younger days that she's not taking into her thirties. No way.

Now that I'm twenty-nine I'm becoming a new kind of woman, the kind who gets married to the guy who gets her pregnant, not the kind who keeps the pregnancy a secret and ends one when she discovers her boyfriend is cheating, and ends another when the gray-eyed tourist goes back to his home in Mexico, and ends the third when her boyfriend of nine weeks goes on a fishing trip with his buddies.

Okay, there are things I've done that I'm not proud of, and abortions may or may not be at the top of my list, but really, truly, I only remember feeling relief, like I'd had a bad tooth removed or a blister popped—I mean, cramps and all, I felt lighter afterwards, and was grateful to the people who helped me out, the doctor who stuttered and spit when he talked, the nurse who held my hand until I lost consciousness—but I'm trying not to think about them today.

I'm driving with my husband Jimmy and we're on our way to Laughlin, where Jimmy's dad teaches math at Laughlin Junior College during the day and deals cards at night. Jimmy wants to introduce me to his family before I start showing. He probably shouldn't worry about me showing, though, because I bet there's blood in my underwear right now. I've got cramps and feel damp down there. I'm moving around, uncomfortable in the seat, but trying to be nonchalant.

The truth is I'm afraid that Jimmy is as uncertain about our love as I am about Ludlow, which is where we're stopping, taking the off-ramp to get some gas. "You sure you want to stop here?" I say, but he's already exiting, pointing out the Texaco station on our right and the coffee shop on our left, which has a sign that's actually visible from the off-ramp itself. It says EAT in big, blinking red letters. "We can get some food too," he says. "We'll stop a while and stretch our legs. Let's eat at EAT," he says, laughing.

"It's not called EAT," I say.

"It's fun to say, though. Try it. *Let's eat at EAT.*"

I shake my head.

"Come on."

"Let's eat at EAT," I say, smiling. "It is sort of fun, Jimmy."

"James," he says. "Remember?"

"Oh yeah," I say, "James. James. James."

Jimmy has wanted me to call him James for the last six weeks, since he started his job as a paralegal, because he says that a lawyer shouldn't be called Jimmy.

"But you're not a lawyer," I said, which was obviously the wrong thing to say, because Jimmy scowled. "Not yet, I mean."

"That's right."

"But you *will* be."

"Damn straight, Dar. Once I get into a good law school."

"Don't you have to get some other degree first?"

"I've got a few classes left."

I looked at him.

"Okay," he said. "Maybe five or six."

"You'll buzz through them, Jimmy."

"*James,*" he corrected.

"That's right, James," and the name James felt silly coming out of my mouth, like I was talking to someone else.

While Jimmy pumps the gas I go to the bathroom, expecting to mop up a mess. I stand impatiently eyeing the metal tampon box on the wall with my legs together, my dollar poised. I give a smile to the young mother with her little boy at the sink. She's showing him how to wash his hands, helping him. She pushes the silver button and that grainy pink powder falls from the spout into her palm, and then she's putting the powder on his little hands and then cupping them. With both of her hands on top of his, she's rubbing, gently it looks like, but he still says, *ouch,* still winces, but then he's giggling, and what might be a touching sight on any other day is making my stomach hurt, and I'm wishing she'd get the boy cleaned up fast and get the fuck out of here so that I can just buy what I need. I'm smiling at the woman, though, because I feel like I have to—I give her a tight, insincere smile, thinking, *hurry the fuck up.*

"Come on, Raymond," Mommy finally says, "let's go." She looks at me then like I'm the devil and she's got to protect her son from me and my kind. She's hiding little Raymond behind her floral skirt or maybe he's hiding himself, afraid on his own, already aware of the kind of woman I so obviously am.

When I'm finally alone I buy both a tampon and a pad. I go into the first stall and am met by one lone turd floating in the water, probably the boy's, I'm thinking, or better yet Mommy's, and it gives me a little rush to think of her hiking up her pretty skirt and leaving it. I move to the next stall. I check myself out before I pee. I've really got to pee, though, and it takes will and bladder strength to hold it. I'm standing with my legs and knees apart. I pull on the crotch of my white cotton panties and look for signs—the smallest spot of blood. Nothing. Not one red drop. I'm surprised, but the day's anything but over. Darlene's got a feeling and her feeling says that this is the day she's going to lose the baby, and that it serves her right for having all those abortions and for not feeling guilty about having them. That it's just what she deserves for forgetting to take her pill and then forgetting to tell Jimmy she forgot.

I'm washing my own hands now with that cheap soap, and I see what I think is a towel on the floor in the corner, but when I stretch my neck and look closer, I notice it's a diaper stained yellow with piss. I dry my hands with that awful brown paper that gas stations use and stare at myself in the mirror. I look okay, sort of pale maybe, so I get out my blush and put on a little extra.

When I get to the car, Jimmy is sitting in the front seat smoking. He takes a long, last drag, and the cigarette sizzles and shrinks. He tosses it out the window before I get inside. "You hungry?"

"No," I say, "but I could use a cup of coffee."

"I want you to eat at EAT," he says, laughing.

It's not so funny to me this time. If I had written a list for Jimmy, it would have started with: *It bugs me when you beat a joke to death.*

"Good girl." He starts the car and pulls out into the street, and I'm thinking that the second thing on my list would have read: *It bugs me when you say, Good girl.*

"It's like nowhere out here," I say. "Who lives here? Every-one is so damn white."

"We're white," Jimmy says.

"Yeah, but everyone's not white where we live."

"Diversity, Darlene—you're a good woman and you like diversity." He's nodding and smiling.

"I guess so."

He drives with one hand on the wheel and rubs his neck with the other.

"You tired?" I ask him.

"No," he says. "I think I just pulled a muscle. Must have slept funny last night." He winks at me.

"Last night?"

"You remember last night, don't you?"

"Yeah, but Darlene didn't—"

"Didn't what?"

"You were so . . ." I begin, and then change my mind.

"What?"

"Forget it."

"Tell me," he says.

I look out the window and say nothing.

"So *what*, Dar?"

I turn back and look at him. "You know, gentle."

He laughs then. "Really?"

"Sort of."

"I'll be better tonight. I guess I'm just nervous about the baby," he says.

"Let me drive the next stretch, Jimmy—I mean, James. If your neck hurts."

"I like driving," he says.

Jimmy's not mean and he's not a cheat and he's never given me any reason not to believe him. And if you happen to be in one of the cars we pass along the highway, you would look in and see us, a couple, in Jimmy's red truck, his hand on my thigh, and his puffy, sweet lips pursed because he's whistling, which might mean that he's even happy we're married and about to have a baby, but I can't help thinking that it's the baby he loves, a baby he hopes is a boy, and that I'm the thing housing the boy, and without *him,* Jimmy wouldn't need a house, he'd do just as fine in a one-room apartment.

I've never told him about my mother and my mother's mother, how their first several pregnancies ended in sobs, in bloody cloths and midnight trips to the hospital. I haven't told him about that bitch psychic either. And I haven't uttered a word about the men who came before him—and there were plenty.

I worked the desk in a fancy hotel downtown for most of my twenties, and several of those men were tourists, away from home and only in town for a short while. They moved, with my help and insistence, I'll admit, through my life and body as easily as they moved from city to city. What I'm trying to say is that almost everyone I've ever been with has been on his way somewhere else, and because of who he was, what he was willing or not willing to sacrifice, in addition to the things I did and said, the way I laughed or crossed my legs, the way I talked about big plans of my own that didn't include him, he'd only be stopping through. Like Ludlow—I'm like Ludlow itself—and though Jimmy's enjoying his cheeseburger and fries, licking his fingers, and making those little sighs he makes when he's loving a meal, he'll be happy when we're back in the truck and on our way out of here.

• • •

One man who *wasn't* on his way anywhere—actually, he was a boy then, my very first boy—was Mickey Hunter, and despite what he said about me, I was not a crazy, jealous, paranoid girl, and I didn't give the worst head in the world—well, okay, perhaps I was a little timid, but I was only nineteen. And even though I wasn't sure I loved Mickey, I did want him to love *me*, if not for forever like he promised, then at least until we graduated from junior college.

I was working at Pretzel Palace in the mall, and Mickey worked across the way at The Cheese House. Everything they served there was dipped in this salty orange sauce: apples, hot dogs, mini-loaves of sourdough. Mickey's job was to keep the cheese sauce creamy; he continually stirred the huge vat. Imagine a fondue pot the size of a trash can and imagine a spoon the size of a small oar and you've got a picture of Mickey at work. He'd stop stirring only to wipe his brow with a cloth or to wave and blow me a kiss.

I'd been at Pretzel Palace for six months, going out with Mickey for five, and the waving and kissing had nearly stopped, and my period was eight days late when a girl came bouncing into the store to buy a pretzel. Her name tag said *Hi, I'm Candy* and I hated her instantly, and believe it or not, she worked at the Chocolate Factory two stores down. Candy wore a brown uniform—brown shorts, tight brown T-shirt, brown tennis shoes, and even a silly brown cowboy hat. "It's too bad you have to wear all brown. Kind of drab, huh?" I said.

"It's not brown, it's *coco beige*," she said, all snotty.

"Whatever," I said.

Candy rolled her eyes, which were also *coco beige*, and put a dollar and two quarters on the counter for a Jumbo Plain. "Easy on the salt," she told me.

I watched her walk with her pretzel over to The Cheese House and I knew from the haughty bounce in her step, and from the quick glance back she gave me midway, that she not only liked my Mickey but knew he was mine, and that this made him all the more alluring to her, which meant that the two of them had discussed me. She stood, cocky, her neck bent to one side so that her cowboy hat hit her shoulder. She adjusted and readjusted that stupid hat and laughed loud enough for me to hear.

Mickey was stirring his cheese sauce and glancing over at me to see if I was looking over at the two of them, which I obviously was. Still, he took the pretzel from her hand and in one grossly gallant, sweeping motion dipped it into the trash can full of cheese—which was, by the way, breaking store rules. A sign on the wall said: *We Only Dip What You Buy Here.*

He held the now-orange pretzel with a tiny tissue and handed it back to Candy, telling me with the gesture that not only did she like him, but that he liked her too, and that the two of them had probably already fucked.

"Hey, traitor," I shouted. "Hey you two," I said. "I know what's happening, you cheese-eating whore."

Neither one of them looked back at me. "I'm going to kick your chocolate ass. Get over here, Candy, so I can kick your ass, you chocolate bitch," I shouted, and then I was trying to make my way to them without, for some reason, using the door. I was crawling up onto the counter, my knees smashing pretzels—cinnamon pretzels, garlic pretzels, and Italian herb pretzels. I didn't make it, though, was stopped by my boss's big hand on my shoulder, who up until this point had always been very nice. "You're out of here, Darlene," he said. "No more Pretzel Palace for you," he told me.

Three weeks later I drove myself to my first abortion, lied to the nurse, telling her that my fiancé Michael Hunter, who works in the restaurant business, would be picking me up in the parking lot right after the procedure, so it was okay, fine, to put me out, put me under. "Knock me out," I said.

I remember driving myself home, still fucked up and probably hormonally depressed, thinking, sadly, angrily, that a girl's beginning decides everything that happens next. I doubt now that it would have made a difference in the woman I've become, but sometimes I wonder what I'd be like if Mickey Hunter had been faithful or had broken up with me in a more reasonable way. Like maybe we'd have been sitting side by side on his porch step or my porch step, his hand on my knee and he'd have been lying, sure, but letting me down gently, saying, "I care about you a lot, Darlene, but we're young, really young, and I need some space." And then I would have confessed that my period was late and that it had never been late before, and he would have said, "What, you're pregnant?" and not with a mean voice, but a concerned one. "I'll help you out—it's your body, whatever you want to do, I'm here . . ."

Our waitress, who introduced herself to us moments ago as the coffee shop's owner, is about sixty. Her name is Darlene too, which embarrasses me for some reason, but she's pleasant with a big smile and friendly manner, and does a good job keeping my coffee cup filled. Jimmy smiles at Darlene when she goes to pour and looks up to make sure that the lip of the pot is green and not orange which means I'm getting decaf. "The little things are important, Dar," he says, "like getting a good night's sleep and drinking decaf, staying away from cigarette smoke and going for a walk now and then."

I'm nodding and picking at the lettuce leaves, which poke out from underneath my hamburger bun. The burger is half eaten, which is as much as I can take right now, and I haven't touched the fries. They sit in a big, glistening heap on the plate in front of me.

"Come on, eat something. Eat at EAT," Jimmy says, coming in toward me with a couple shoestring potatoes between two fingers. "Come on, Dar," he tries.

"No," I say.

"You still nauseous?"

"Sort of."

He looks sad a minute and then perks right up, putting the fries in his own mouth. "I was thinking that I'd quit smoking before the baby comes," he says, chewing.

"Good idea."

"In fact, I'm going to make the cigarette I smoke after this burger the last one ever," he says.

"Darlene doesn't feel so good, Jimmy."

"Let's get you a soda, something with bubbles." He twists in the booth and waves at the other Darlene, who comes right over. "Can we get a 7-up?" he asks her.

"Right away," she says.

"You feel really bad, Dar?"

"Yeah."

"Can I eat your burger, then?" He's leaning over, reaching for it, before I can even answer.

Darlene sets the soda in front of me. "Anything else?"

"Thanks, no," Jimmy says. "Great burger."

The psychic's name was Brick and this is what she said: you are worthy of love and happiness but will not find it now, not this time. There's a fetus in you that's about to die.

"What?" I said, thinking maybe I'd heard wrong.

"There's a fetus in you that's about to die," she said again, in a voice so high and squeaky that any news, no matter how serious, would sound like good news.

"About to die?" I said.

"Yes, on Tuesday, this coming Tuesday," she squeaked, "the fetus will quit."

"Quit?" I said. "It's not like he has a job, lady."

"The fetus is going to quit," she repeated.

"What's he doing, selling shoes or serving coffee in my uterus?"

Brick shook her head.

"You don't know a damn thing about Darlene Tate. Don't know what in the hell you're talking about. You're crazy."

"I am crazy, yes, but I do know what I'm talking about. I know about babies," she said.

I got really mad then, stood up, and started gathering my

things, my sweater and bag, and if there'd been someone to complain to I would have done it. But to who? I mean, I visited a woman who lives under a bridge, who'd made a house for herself out of boxes. I'd been sitting on a cube of red bricks—hence her name—she'd called a seat.

"He's a she," Brick said then.

"What?"

"*He* is a *she*. You're carrying a girl," she told me.

"Fuck you," I said, walking away from her and her bridge.

Okay, besides being Jimmy's idea of a baby killer, I'm gullible. He should have written on that list: *It bugs me that you're gullible.* I was muttering all the way to my car and even thought about turning around and going back to her, picking up one of those bricks I'd been sitting on, and hitting her over the head with it, but I'm not a killer, no matter what Jimmy would think about my abortions.

We're the only people in Darlene's diner and I'm looking around, wondering how she stays in business. Black-and-white photographs of cowboys line the wall on my left—men in boots and big hats, like the brown one Candy from the Chocolate Factory wore, one guy spinning a rope in the air, a little girl, with someone I assume is her father, sitting on a dark pig. The mountains outside are brown and gray, rolling into one another so that you can't tell where one ends and another begins. I'm thinking about the way Jimmy made love to me last night, carefully and without confidence, not his style. I didn't like it, him on top of me, completely supporting himself with both arms, so that I couldn't feel his body's weight at all. Him entering me so slowly and gently that I didn't recognize him. *Relax,* I wanted to say. *Let's do it like we did it last month, like lovers. Let's do it like the night we met.*

Jimmy's like his dad, good with numbers and good at cards, especially blackjack. He's good at games in general, backgammon and darts and pool, which is what he was playing that first night. He was out with his brother Eddie, winning every game. Eddie was cussing and sneering, Jimmy was that good. He hit this ball, which flew to the left and hit that ball, which bounced against the edge of the table and hit a third ball, and Jimmy was glowing. In between fine shots like that one he'd look over at me and take a swig of his beer and smile. It was like we were already a team, in that game of pool together, though I was sitting clear across the room on a stool and didn't yet know him. I'd noticed him as soon as I walked into the bar, though, even pointed him out to Annie.

I loved watching Jimmy win, his fingers curling around the cue stick, his sparkly dark eyes, his concentration, and all that confidence. It stirred me up, and I was nudging Annie to get us another beer and maybe a couple shots of vodka because that way I'd have enough nerve to approach Jimmy or maybe I'd look at him long and hard enough until he approached me, which is what he finally did.

· · ·

Darlene isn't just the waitress and owner, but the cashier as well. I wouldn't be surprised if it was she who flipped our burgers and toasted our buns. She stands behind the cash register now, twirling her wedding ring. In an ankle-length pink-and-white checkered dress and an apron, with her red hair done up in a fat bun, she looks like she's from another time, old-fashioned, the way people look out here. She stares hopefully out the front window, across the street at a car that's pulled into the gas station. She's wondering if they're hungry too, I'm certain, hoping that maybe their bodies need fuel, too.

A man steps out into the dirt. He stretches and yawns. He kicks a rock at his feet. "I wonder if he's hungry," I say without thinking.

"What? Who?" Jimmy says, turning around in the booth to look at the guy.

"I wonder if EAT gets enough business, I mean."

Jimmy shrugs, then picks up the last of my burger. He puts it in his mouth, then takes a sip of his Coke. He leans back against the booth and exhales. He stares at me. "You're so damn pretty, Darlene," he says.

"No," I say. "Not really."

"You are too. And you're also a good woman, which is even more important."

"Darlene Tate's not a good woman," I say, surprising myself. "There are things I've done, Jimmy. You wouldn't approve of the things I've done." And then I'm almost crying and Jimmy's scooting over in the booth so that his body is right next to mine.

191

"I don't need to know what you've done, Dar."

I'm shaking my head, sniffling.

"I need to know what you're *going to do*," he says. "What we're going to do together."

I pick up the napkin in front of me and blow my nose. "Okay," I say. "Okay, Jimmy—I mean, James."

I went to that psychic because Annie had heard that the woman was the best in town and that she specialized in pregnancy. Annie called her gifted, said she could tell me what my baby's gender was, and if he'd have green eyes, blue eyes, or brown, and—if I wanted, for a few extra dollars—on what day of the week he'd be born. She could tell me if the epidural would work or if my labor would still hurt like hell. That was also Brick's specialty—predictions about pain. She had, according to my friend, an uncanny ability to tell you whether you'll breeze through labor or if you'd better brace yourself. "Watch," Annie had said, "one day that woman is going to be on Larry King."

If she's so damn talented, I should have asked Annie, then why does she live under the 405 Freeway?

Jimmy and I are standing together holding hands in front of Darlene's cash register. She's looking down at our check and adding things up in her head. "You've got my wife's name," Jimmy says, smiling.

Darlene nods and smiles back at him. "Where you two headed?"

"Laughlin," Jimmy tells her. "My new wife's going to meet my father."

"Your daddy lives there?"

"He teaches at the J.C."

"J.C.?"

"Junior College," I chime in.

"And he's a dealer. Blackjack," Jimmy says.

"You a dealer too?" Darlene wants to know.

"No," he says. "I'm going to be a lawyer."

"Wow," she says.

"He's real smart," I tell her.

Darlene smiles, counts three dollars' change into Jimmy's palm.

"I'm feeling lucky," he says. "We're going to strike it rich."

"Be careful," Darlene says. "My third husband lost everything out there. Came home with absolutely nothing. Left in our Dodge Dart and came home on the bus." Darlene shakes her head.

"We're going to have a baby," Jimmy says, letting go of my hand so that he can put his arm around my shoulder. He pulls me to him a little too hard. I wriggle away and leave Jimmy and Darlene to talk about my future while I head to the bathroom.

Then I'm standing in the stall, staring once again at the crotch of my underwear, looking for signs of trouble. Again, nothing—white, clean cotton.

Maybe it'll happen while we're in Laughlin, and Jimmy's making some money at the blackjack table.

Maybe I'll be huddled up somewhere in the hotel, bleeding.

I stand there a minute, thinking of that first night with Jimmy and all the nights that have come after. I think about how much I love him and it occurs to me that he might love me too the way he says he does, and that he might continue to love me even if that psychic is right. But she's not right yet, so I pull up my underwear and go out to meet Jimmy, who's now standing by the car, smoking his last cigarette.

I thought that if I went to the psychic I'd at least have something to talk about at parties, a story to tell. I did this once, I wanted to say, and she said this and this and that and it all came true. Or, she didn't know a Goddamn thing—what a waste of fifty bucks. I'm hoping it's the latter and I'm hoping Jimmy's dad likes me and I'm hoping that if I get to be a mother this time around I'll be a good one.

When Jimmy sees me walking toward him, he drops the cigarette to the dirt and smashes it with his shoe, sending the tiniest dust cloud into the air. He opens the door for me and I climb into the truck. When I go to turn on the radio, Jimmy puts his hand over my hand. "No music," he says, "let's just talk. I want to hear everything you have to say, Dar. You're my wife."

Acknowledgments

I am grateful to many people and organizations: to Yaddo, MacDowell, Fundación Valparaiso, and the California Arts Council for the gift of time and support. To Martin Miller and the *Los Angeles Times*, for the article "Bright Flash. Bad Luck. Or Bad Karma," which inspired my short story "The Study of Lightning Injury." To Marilyn Johnson, Leelila Strogov, and David Hernandez, who read my short stories and offered their intelligence and tact. To my loyal agent Andrew Blauner, who doesn't stop, who said he would *open the door* and who did, and who's now going for the hinges. And finally, to Tara Parsons, always a joy, and David Rosenthal at Simon & Schuster—and a special thank you to my very talented editor Marysue Rucci.

About the Author

Lisa Glatt was awarded the 2003 Mississippi Review Prize in Fiction and recently received a writing fellowship from the Civitella Ranieri Center in Italy. Her work has appeared in various publications, including *Zoetrope, Columbia, Indiana Review, Swink*, and on Nerve.com. Lisa lives in Long Beach, California, with her husband, the poet and writer David Hernandez. Visit her website at www.lisaglatt.com.

Also available from Lisa Glatt
The National Bestseller

0-7432-5776-6

"An appealingly dark first novel . . . authentic, substantial and engaging."
—*The New York Times Book Review*

"Smart and stylish. . . . Lyrical and sophisticated."
—*San Francisco Chronicle*

"*A Girl Becomes a Comma Like That* adds an emphatic exclamation point to the start of a promising career."
—*Vanity Fair*

SIMON & SCHUSTER
PAPERBACKS
A VIACOM COMPANY

Visit www.simonsays.com